CROW

CROW

Barbara Wright

Random House 🏠 New York

Text copyright © 2012 by Barbara Wright
Jacket art copyright © 2012 by Edel Rodriguez

Visit us on the Web! www.randomhouse.com/kids

Educators and librarians, for a variety of teaching tools, visit us at www.randomhouse.com/teachers

Library of Congress Cataloging-in-Publication Data
Wright, Barbara.
Crow / Barbara Wright. — 1st ed.
p. cm.
Summary: In 1898, Moses Thomas's summer vacation does not go exactly as planned as he contends with family problems and the ever-changing alliances among his friends at the same time as he is exposed to the escalating tension between the African American and white communities of Wilmington, North Carolina.
ISBN 978-0-375-86928-0 (trade) — ISBN 978-0-375-96928-7 (lib. bdg.)
ISBN 978-0-375-98270-5 (ebook) — ISBN 978-0-375-87367-6 (pbk.)
1. African Americans—Juvenile fiction. 2. Wilmington (N.C.)—History—19th century—Juvenile fiction. [1. African Americans—Fiction. 2. Wilmington (N.C.)—History—19th century—Fiction. 3. Family life—North Carolina—Fiction. 4. Friendship—Fiction. 5. Race relations—Fiction.] I. Title.
PZ7.W932Cr 2012 [Fic]—dc23 2011014892

Printed in the United States of America
10 9 8 7 6 5 4 3 2 1
First Edition

For Julius

ONE

The buzzard knew. He gave the first warning. I was playing in the backyard while my grandmother stirred the iron wash pot over the fire. She had gray hair and a bent back. Standing, she looked like the left-hand side of a Y. If she'd been able to straighten her back, she would have been taller than me, but since she couldn't, we were the same height. I called her Boo Nanny. She joked that I should call her Bent Granny.

She took in wash from white people in town. In our backyard, clotheslines were stretched four feet off the ground. A higher line held pants and sheets. Daddy had built a platform so she could reach.

The morning of my last day of fifth grade, the weather was hot—not as hot as it would get in a few weeks, when sand scalded bare feet and doors swelled so much that it was hard to open them, but hot enough so that the salt breeze from the ocean did little to cool things off. Boo

Nanny wore a cabbage leaf on her head to protect her from the sun. Holding the cupped green leaf to her head with one hand, she shaded her eyes and looked up into the sky, clear but for some feathery clouds in the shape of seagull wings.

Several birds looped around in the high currents, too far away to cast a shadow. They were black and shiny like crows, but as awkward as flying turkeys. Their wings held fixed, the birds did the dead man's float in the air, drifting in lazy figure eights around an invisible circle but never running into each other.

Then one lit out from the group and swooped down, pulling its shadow across the yard, over the top edges of the clothes on the line.

Suddenly Boo Nanny shoved me onto the sand and covered my body with hers. The cabbage leaf flew off to the side. Her bent back made her look fragile, but in fact she was strong from hauling heavy irons from the fire and taking water from the well to the pit for boiling wash. Still, I was startled by how fast she could move.

"What's wrong?" I said, alarmed, feeling the weight of her thin body on mine.

"Buzzard's shadow," Boo Nanny said, rolling off me and struggling to her feet. "That old thing tag you, means you happiness done dead."

"Did he get me?" I asked, worried. "Did you see?"

"I don't know. If he do, a mess of trouble be headed to our door," she said.

Before Boo Nanny tackled me, I had watched the buzzard break off from the circle and glide down toward us. The flat gray shape beneath it bent and unfolded as the buzzard passed over the fence and slipped away from us.

I didn't notice if the shadow had grazed my head or skimmed over any part of me. But I couldn't say for absolute sure that I hadn't been tagged. The shadow left no outward sign. What if I was a marked boy and didn't even know it? But I was more worried about Boo Nanny. She had protected me by covering my body with hers, and if the shadow had grazed anyone, it was her.

I went to school and didn't think any more about the morning's events, but the buzzard's shadow opened up inside me a pinhole of dread. On the last day of class, the students were fidgety. Everyone was ready for summer to begin. Everyone, that is, except for me. Who would help Miss Annie with the buckets when it rained in the summer? That was my job during the year. The roof leaked, and the bare walls and ceiling of the second floor were covered with stains the color of tobacco spit. We kept the maps and phonetic charts on the first floor, where it stayed dry.

At the awards ceremony that afternoon, I received a certificate for perfect attendance. I was so excited, I couldn't wait until evening and had to show my father that very afternoon. He was proud of how smart I was.

My father was a reporter for the Wilmington *Daily Record*, the only Negro daily in the South. The offices were located on the corner of Princess and Water Streets, across from the wharf. After school, I walked along Market Street, lined with live oaks whose great spreading branches drooped with hanks of wiry gray moss that Boo Nanny called haint's hair. As I walked along, I leaped up to touch the moss, being careful not to damage my attendance certificate, which I had placed on the back of my slate and secured with a book strap.

At Front Street, white ladies in hats and white gloves exited the streetcar and held their long skirts above the muck left by mules, horses, and oxen. A block farther on, I turned right and walked by the wharf, where the three-masted schooners and steamships were docked along the Cape Fear River.

The air, softened by salt moisture, was crowded with noisy gulls waiting for scraps from the fish vendors. Men sold hot biscuits and fried bananas from carts, while coon dogs and the occasional shoat milled about.

I rarely visited Daddy at work, but today was a special day. I smoothed the edges of my certificate against my slate and felt happy, imagining how proud he would be.

At the *Record* office, I took the outside stairs, past the

first-floor saloon with a sign that read: WHOEVER DRINKS HERE—RETURN FOR ANOTHER DRAUGHT. Even this early in the day, the place was crowded and noisy. I was under strict instructions from my mother to stay away from the saloon, which was not a problem. I liked the sound of white sailors singing off-key, but the smell of pickles and sawdust made my stomach turn.

On the second floor, I didn't see Daddy at his desk and asked the first man I saw where I could find him.

"Ask Alex Manly. He'll know your father's whereabouts," the clerk said, and pointed to a white man across the room. He was tall and had black hair, but not the way my hair was black. His was soft and straight and thin and lay flat on his head, like a horse's coat.

I looked around for someone else. I was certain that the owner of the largest colored paper in the state would not be a white man, though I knew that many white companies advertised in the paper.

"That's Mr. Manly?" I asked.

"Yes, he'll know where your father is."

"That's okay," I said, and turned to leave, too shy to ask the white man a question.

But before I got out the door, he came over and said, "Can I help you?"

"I'm Moses, Jack Thomas's son."

I looked Mr. Manly straight in the eye and gave him

an extra firm handshake, like Daddy had taught me. "A good grip shows you're the equal of any man," Daddy always said. "Now show me some pride. If you give me that seaweed grip, I'm going to think you're cowed and ashamed."

I gave the white man my best grip, and it worked. He did not look down at my shoes. On that score, I had come up short. Well-shined shoes were also a sign of character, according to Daddy. "In college, I shined my shoes every day," he had said.

He still did, every evening before going to bed. I loved my daddy, but I drew the line at polishing my shoes. Many of the children in the younger grades didn't even wear shoes. If I showed up with shoes as shiny as Daddy's, I'd be laughed out of school.

The white man said, "Your father's out covering a story but should be back shortly. In the meantime, would you like to see our new printing press?"

"Yessir," I said, aware that everything I did reflected on my father.

Mr. Manly explained that when the paper converted from a weekly to a daily, he had purchased on installment a four-cylinder Hoe rotary press from the editor of the *Wilmington Messenger*, the white newspaper.

Tongue-tied, I followed Mr. Manly down a narrow hall. It was sad—a boy with a perfect attendance record couldn't think of one intelligent thing to say. Luckily, when we entered the back room, the thundering noise made talking impossible.

In the center of the room, the press churned out printed pages in stacks that got higher and higher with each rotation. The mighty machine had as many moving parts as a locomotive.

The air in the room was stifling and smelled of machine oil and ink. Four boys not much older than me fed paper into the four smaller cylinders placed around the giant cylinder at the center. Their sweat-soaked shirts clung to their narrow chests, and ink smudges stained their skin. I wondered why the boys weren't in school.

Flies buzzed around the room. Using my slate as a fan, I waved them away, but the boys at the press, with their hands occupied, could only toss their heads like horses, without the benefit of a tail to get rid of the pests.

The boy closest to me had a burred scalp interrupted by squiggly lines of no hair, like you'd find on worm-eaten shells. He looked up briefly at my clean clothes and slate and glowered as if to say, "Sissy." The look passed in a split second. Any longer, and his fingers would have been drawn into the hungry machine.

I wouldn't want to meet these boys on the wharf after work. They would beat me up, for sure. Well, I didn't care what they thought. I wasn't a sissy. I was small for my age, but quick and athletic, and I could outrun them if need be—though I didn't feel like putting my abilities to the test.

"This is quite a machine!" Mr. Manly shouted.

"Yessir, it is," I said.

I could feel the machine vibrating through the soles of my feet. I watched in awe as the press slurped the pages into its innards and spit them out onto cast-iron beds, inked on both sides, ready to be wrapped in twine and delivered by wagon across the state.

"Prints eight thousand copies an hour," Mr. Manly said.

The number seemed unimaginably huge. I wondered how many Negroes there were in North Carolina, in the world.

When we went back to the office, my ears were still ringing. Daddy was at his desk.

Mr. Manly said, "That's a fine young man you've got there, Jack."

I looked down shyly, but felt proud to be praised by someone as important as Mr. Manly. I noticed he'd called me a man, and not a boy.

"Yes, he is," Daddy said, beaming. "Today is a big day for him. I do believe he has passed into the sixth grade."

I grinned. I wanted to bring up my perfect attendance record, but didn't want to brag in front of Mr. Manly.

"This calls for a treat," Daddy said. He looked at Mr. Manly for permission and received an agreeable nod.

We went outside to the wharf and Daddy bought me a corn cake from a stout woman with a flat basket on her head. We continued along Water Street, where skippers mingled with smartly dressed brokers, arranging for passage of goods. The wharf was filled with jostling and sweating and shouting as Negroes and South Americans loaded pine and cypress timbers, burlap bags of rice, and barrels of turpentine, resin, and pitch onto steamers.

"Why is the editor a white man?" I asked, and bit into the cake. The sweetness burst inside my mouth.

"He's a Negro. He just looks white," Daddy said.

"Like Mama."

"You know she'd have your hide if she heard you say that." Mules and wagons clopped loudly along the cobblestone street. "So, tell me, what did you think of the printing press?" Daddy said.

"It was big and loud," I said. It had been thrilling to watch the power of the thundering cylinder transform blank paper into a newspaper, with headlines and articles.

"Yes, we're proud of it, even if it's not the latest model. The press allows us to print the paper daily instead of weekly, and deliver it statewide. Our people will be better citizens and vote more intelligently if they are informed about the issues. That makes for a stronger democracy."

"What about people who can't read?" I asked, licking my fingers so no crumbs went to waste.

"That's why education is so important."

"I bet those filthy chowderheads can't read," I said. "They don't even go to school."

"Who?"

"Those boys my age feeding paper into the press."

Daddy stopped walking and turned to face me. His voice became stern. "Moses, don't ever make fun of people less fortunate than you. There's nothing to be gained by it."

"I didn't mean to . . . I was only . . . Who cares about a few stupid boys?" The corn cake broke in my hand and fell onto the cobbles.

"You aren't necessarily smarter than they are—just luckier."

Shame flared up inside me. I felt terrible for what I had said.

"Son, those boys probably have to work to support their families. Try to put yourself in their skin, look at the world from their point of view."

When I did, all I could think of was how I'd like to beat up a little smarty like me for feeling superior.

I felt tears forming, and that made me angry. I swatted

at the edge of my eye, as if getting rid of a skeeter. More than anything in the world, I hated disappointing my father. I couldn't bear to look at him.

"Hey, I didn't mean to make you feel bad. Today's a big day. You're a sixth grader. In the blink of an eye, you're going to be grown and off to college."

I smiled, but didn't mean it. Luckily, he had to get back to work, so I bid him good-bye and continued along the wharf beyond the boats to an open spot by the river. I removed my perfect attendance certificate from the back of my slate, ripped it up, and flung it into the air. The pieces fluttered down and scattered upon the water. I watched as the swift current carried them down the Cape Fear River, toward the ocean and the wide world beyond.

When I got home, Boo Nanny was outside taking laundry from the line. Usually I had no trouble filling my time, but this afternoon I felt at loose ends, and summer vacation wasn't even a day old. I felt too restless to read. The swamp was filled with thick vines to swing on. I could poke around the sweet-water streams choked with lily pads and black snaky roots. Or I could go digging for clams and oysters in the marshes outside of town. But I didn't feel like doing any of that.

What I really wanted to do was whack at something.

I picked up the stick Boo Nanny used to beat the clothes on a stump by the fire pit after she boiled them. She called it her battling stick—"battling the clothes to cleanliness." The thick wood was worn smooth from so much use. I stretched out under the high line of sun-starched sheets, squinting at the sky.

The clouds were going by so swiftly, they gave the impression that the earth itself was moving, and me along with it. I thumped the wooden stick against the hanging sheets as I considered how nice it would be if my small patch of ground actually was moving and could take me away from this spot, the way schooners took cotton and peanuts and turpentine to lands across the ocean.

Boo Nanny spread apart two sheets, and her head appeared at the opening.

"What's wrong with my baby chile?" she asked.

"Nothing," I said.

"Don't tell me nothing, like I ain't got eyes in my head. You come slinking back from school, puny as the law allows."

"I don't feel so good," I said, tapping at the bottom of the sheet.

She placed her palm on my forehead.

"I don't mean sick," I said, before she could give me one of her potions.

She often took me along with her to hunt for plants in the longleaf pine forest. She knew which part of each plant had healing properties. It could be the bark, the leaves, the roots, the berries, the flowers, the hips, or the stalks. She knew which plants flowered every other year, and which season was the best for collecting. I loved going with her, but I hated the potions she cooked up. The smell alone was enough to make me sick.

Daddy was a modern man and didn't believe in the old slave ways.

"She never gets colds," I pointed out.

"No wonder. With that nasty-smelling pouch she wears around her neck in cold season, people keep their distance, and germs don't get anywhere near her," he said.

Now Boo Nanny looked at me hard. "Well, you got good color. I reckon ain't nothing wrong with you a little strawberry pie couldn't cure." She took the battling stick away from me. "I better fix you up afore you set my wash to ruination," she said.

I followed her into the kitchen. She always had a pie cooling behind the tin doors of the pie safe, punctured with little holes in flower shapes to let air through. You could tell what season it was by the pies she made, starting in spring with strawberry and rhubarb, following through the summer with raspberry, blueberry, blackberry, and

cherry, then entering autumn with apple, grape, pumpkin, and yam.

She took out the leftover strawberry pie and gave me
the next-to-last piece. I brought it to the back porch and
ate while she returned to work.

Before long, our neighbor Mr. Marsh stopped at the
fence. He had a wiry gray beard that looked like the
moss that drooped from the branches of the live oaks.

"Afternoon, Miss Josephine. How you?" he said.

"Above ground," Boo Nanny said. "How's you and
the missus?"

I slid my pie behind the kindling box. It would be rude
to eat in front of him, and I didn't want Boo Nanny to
offer him the last piece.

"She ain't pert like usual. She took sick to the bed
and has the misery in her side. You got a little something
you can fix her up with?" The neighbors all came to Boo
Nanny to cure what ailed them.

She asked me to help her get a jar down from a high
shelf. Her bedroom looked like a tobacco barn. She
had poles suspended from the ceiling—low, so she
could reach them—and hung flowers, herbs, and roots
to dry. Her bed was pushed to one side to make room
for a table, which held mounds of crushed leaves, seeds,
and flower petals. The blue-tinted Mason jars that
crowded the shelves were filled with crushed leaves,

wrinkled roots, withered pods, and the threadlike insides of flowers that looked like insect parts. A larger jar held a soup of dark brown liquid with bits floating around, like night soil. Nothing was labeled; she couldn't read or write, but she knew exactly which jars she wanted. She pointed, and I pulled a chair over and got the jars down. She shook out some seedpods and dried flowers onto one of Daddy's old newspapers, folded it up, and returned to the backyard.

"Now boil youself up some turnip greens, take the juice, mix this with it, and feed it to the missus for three days. Come back and tell me how she's keeping," she said, and handed Mr. Marsh the packet over the fence.

"Thank you, Miss Josephine."

After he left, Boo Nanny came and sat beside me on the back steps. I spent more time with her than any other adult. Mama kept house for Colonel Gilchrist's family. She left the house early and came back late, but Boo Nanny was always at home. She knew when something was wrong with me.

"That pie ain't perked you up the way I'd hoped," she said, and patted my knee. Her hands were the color of pecans, black spots and all. "No wonder you ain't none too spry, blame hot as it is. Maybe a story will fix you up."

"What kind of story?" I asked.

"A ghost story."

"How am I supposed to get scared in broad daylight?"

"This one ain't scary. This one's to make you laugh."

I had grown up with her stories. I didn't call her Boo Nanny for nothing. She introduced me to the wampus cat, sea serpents, headless haunts, duppies, night doctors, and plat-eyes, spirits worse than ghosts that took over the bodies of animals. Jack-o'-lanterns were bug-eyed, hairy creatures that bounded about like human-sized grasshoppers. Only people born with the veil could see them. Most people could see only the lanterns they carried. When I looked across the Cape Fear and saw bobbing lights, I knew it could be a boat, or it could be a jack-o'-lantern.

One horrible creature, the hag, wriggled out of her skin and flew about at night, jumping her victims and sucking blood out through their noses. "You knows when the hag ride you, 'cause you makes a sound, same like a shivering owl," Boo Nanny said.

Once when I got a bloody nose, I was convinced a hag was riding me. That night, Boo Nanny gave me a saltshaker and told me if I found the hag's crumpled skin under my bed, to sprinkle it with salt so it would sting too much for her to put it back on.

Now, sitting on the top step of the porch with her bent back, Boo Nanny looked ready to tie her shoe. Sandspurs had caught in the hem of her long skirt.

"If you can get through this without smiling, I be giving you the last of the pie," she said.

"Okay, I guess."

We were hours away from the dark-thirty, the half hour before dark when ghosts came out. But I didn't have anything else to do, and I wanted that last piece of pie, so I listened to the story of Aaron Kelly, a man who died and was buried by his widow. Before the coffin was cold in the ground, he slipped out and joined his widow by the cooking fire. She was not happy to see his skull and bones, and tried to coax him back into the grave, but he refused.

"Ain't you miss me?" the skeleton said.

"How'm I gone miss you when you ain't gone yet?"

"Ain't you gone mourn me?"

"How'm I gone mourn you when you still here?"

A week later, a fiddler stopped by to court the widow. Before he could do too much sweet-mouthing, they were joined by her dead husband.

The fiddler had an idea: he would play and make Dead Aaron dance until his skeleton fell apart. So he took out his fiddle and played a tune. Dead Aaron started dancing. First, a rib bone dropped and rolled around like a barrel hoop. Next, a foot bone clattered to the floor, followed by a finger bone.

"Faster, faster," the widow egged on the fiddler.

Boo Nanny told the story in rhyme and had me

tapping my knee and jiggling my foot in time. Mostly I concentrated on not smiling. I wanted that last piece of pie.

> He yellow teeth snappin',
> He elbows a-rappin',
> He jawbone a-flappin',
> Landy, Lawdy, Dead Aaron could prance.

> He arms a-flip-floppin',
> He knee bones a-poppin',
> The dry bones keep droppin',
> Landy, Lawdy, that dead man do dance.

> Till all's left is de head.
> "I's still jiving," it said.

The dancing skull proved too much for the fiddler. He fled from the house and never came back. The widow buried her husband's bones, but word got around, and she never had another suitor.

I almost made it through to the end of the story with a straight face, but something about the image of the skeleton shucking bones as he cut the buck seemed so silly I had to smile. I was hoping Boo Nanny hadn't noticed. But she didn't miss much.

"No pie for you," she said.

"I didn't laugh."

"You smiled. I seen you," she said.

"Just once." I knew she would give in. She spoiled me when Mama wasn't around. Sure enough, she went into the kitchen to fetch the last of the pie.

When she returned, I said, "Where did you learn all these stories?"

"Around the campfire. Growing up."

"When you were a slave?"

She nodded.

Mama had told me that Boo Nanny had worked on a turpentine plantation north of town. "Tell me stories from those times. Real ones, I mean." As I got older, it was the true stories that interested me most.

"Them stories could scare you for true," she said.

"Is that where you learned which plants could heal?"

"We ain't had no doctors," she said, and then stopped herself, as if she had given away too much.

"So what did you do?"

"Quit nattering at me, boy. You's enough to wear a body down."

"One story. Just one," I pleaded.

"Best not wake up them old sorrows," she said. "It's like them haints. Once you stir them out of they bed, they don't go back so easy-like."

"I'm a big boy now," I assured her. "You can't scare me."

"No need to worry your head about those dark times. All that matters is what's a-comin' tomorrow. And you got plenty of tomorrows headed your way—a smart boy like you."

TWO

"Johnny's riding over, then we can go to the parade," Lewis said. It was the first week of summer vacation, and I was over at my best friend Lewis's house. He lived on the rich white side of town, near Colonel Gilchrist's house, where Mama worked.

"Why'd you invite him? He's so . . . young." That was the worst thing I could think of to say about Johnny. He was only going into fifth grade. Both he and Lewis went to the Gregory School, a private academy in a brick building much nicer than my public school, which was made of boards.

At that moment, Johnny rode up on his bike, ringing the bell to announce his arrival.

"Hey," I said.

Without bothering to answer, he turned his back to me and addressed Lewis. "Where are your wheels?" he said.

"Moses is coming along," Lewis said.

What did he mean, "coming along"? It was my idea in the first place. For weeks I'd been looking forward to the inauguration of the Port City's first full-time fire department.

Johnny turned to me with a sneer. "Oh." He made me feel second-rate, even though he was darker and three inches shorter, not to mention a year behind.

"How's he getting there? He doesn't have a bike," Johnny said.

I put my hands in my pockets and looked down. There was nothing I wanted more than a bicycle, but my family couldn't afford one.

"My father said he'd drop us off," Lewis said.

"Suit yourself." He shrugged. "I'm taking my wheels. Maybe I'll see you, maybe I won't. It's a dumb parade anyway." He rode off.

Just because Johnny's father had been appointed by a United States president to be the collector of customs for the Port of Wilmington didn't make him better than everyone else.

Lewis was rich, but he was not at all stuck-up like Johnny "High-and-Mighty" Dancy. Lewis's father owned his very own carriage. My daddy said that Lewis's daddy was the richest Negro in town. Mr. Taylor owned a lot of real estate and a bank that lent money to Negroes so they could buy their own homes. That was how we got our house. Daddy spoke very highly of Mr. Taylor, and I liked him, too.

The parade was only six blocks away, but I was always glad to ride in a carriage. Lewis's father let us off just as the parade was starting, and we found our place among the excited crowds that lined Market Street. A couple of men pulled a brand-new steam engine with red wheels as high as the men's shoulders. An iron frame supported a towering silver cylinder, like an oversized milk jug, so shiny you could hardly stand to look at it in the sun. Firemen in their uniforms followed in a horse-drawn wagon. There were a few black faces among them, and that made me stand up tall with pride. Printed on the side of the wagon were the words I beheld in awe: WILMINGTON HOOK AND LADDER. I imagined how I would look in one of those red uniforms, waving at the cheering crowds.

"I want to be a fireman," Lewis said.

"I do, too," I said.

"I thought of it first."

"We both thought of it at the same time," I said.

"But I was the one who said it first," he said.

"Why can't we both be firemen?" I suggested.

"Okay. Suits me."

After the parade was over—we did not run into

Johnny, thank goodness—Lewis suggested we play pirates. Blackbeard was our favorite. The real Blackbeard lived a long time ago on Ocracoke Island and terrorized people off the coast of Wilmington. Lewis said that Blackbeard had dark skin like ours, but he wasn't a Negro. He was just dark. He braided his black beard and tied the ends with ribbons, just like the hair of my eight-year-old next-door neighbor, Jane, who was always pestering me to play with her. Blackbeard tied his head up in a rag, like so many folks in our neighborhood.

Lewis insisted on being Blackbeard. "You be the first mate," he said.

"I don't want to be the first mate. I want to be Blackbeard."

"Well, can't both of us be Blackbeard."

I gave in, because I wanted Lewis to stay my best friend. By his count, the primary job of the first mate involved running errands for him. He sent me to our house to get old newspapers to make a kite. We had plenty of newspapers. Daddy read them faster than we could burn them or use them up in the privy. When I got the papers, Boo Nanny was in the kitchen ironing. She paused, wiped the sweat from her gray temples, and asked what I was doing. When I told her, she said, "Honey baby, you you own man. If Lewis say jump, you gone hurl you own self off the cliff, just 'cause he say it?"

In our backyard, Lewis and I penciled the outlines of a skull and crossbones, then painted the newsprint black around the lines, so the design showed through in white newsprint. I sacrificed my red handkerchief to tear into pieces for the tail.

I wanted to fly the kite, but Lewis had other ideas. "Let's go find Jacob's Run. Then we can pretend to be slaves escaping," he said.

Legend had it that tunnels ran under the city, where a former creek called Jacob's Run emptied into the Cape Fear River. We had heard that the tunnels were used as a meeting place for runaway slaves, a hidden path for people fleeing the British invasion of Wilmington during the Revolutionary War, and even as a pathway to carry the bodies of yellow fever victims from the Confederate blockade runners to Bellevue Cemetery.

We had tried many times to find the tunnels. Our friend Nellie Parsons lived in a house built before the War Between the States by her great-grandfather, a free black carpenter. She swore that there was a passage leading from the well in the backyard to the tunnels. We had thrown rocks down the dry well, but were too chicken to lower ourselves on ropes and look around.

"This time we're going to use smarts. Your smarts, old man," Lewis said.

"If the tunnel follows the path of the old creek, that

means it must empty into the Cape Fear," I reasoned. "So if we go to the wharf, we might see where it comes out, and then work backwards."

"Exactly what I had in mind," he said. If the plan worked, he'd claim credit.

We walked to the south end of the wharf. The tide was out, and the boats sat lower in the water. Noisy seagulls and crows ambushed the fishmonger, who was gutting the day's catch. Cats circled the wooden bench, scrounging for scraps. Several Negro boys perched at the water's edge with fishing poles. The air smelled of fish and tar.

Four-masted schooners were docked in the slips, bow first. White bags of sugar, like overstuffed pillows, were lashed together, twelve in each pile, waiting to be hoisted on deck. Mingling among the workmen were merchants, dressed in suits and ties despite the sweltering heat.

I walked along the edge of the dock, looking for clues. I saw reeds at the shoreline, along with a yellow froth, the color of foaming yeast. Fish nipped at the refuse the fishmonger emptied into the water. I could hear the water sloshing under the dock, but I could see no evidence of a stream feeding into the river.

The idea of a passageway hidden beneath the cobbles and pavers intrigued me. But nothing held Lewis's attention for long. By the time we reached Lippitt Ice

House, he had lost interest. We paused on the dock to watch a schooner unload the ice that had been cut from ponds in New England in the winter and stored there until summer, when it was delivered down south. In port, the ice traveled on cables that stretched directly from the ship's deck over Water Street to the second story of Lippitt Ice House. The giant blocks were covered in sawdust and straw, with patches melted away to reveal a glossy surface that reflected the blue of the sky.

Lewis wanted to stand underneath the blocks and wait for the melt-off to cool his skin.

"Betcha I can catch more drops than you," he said.

He made everything into a contest.

I didn't want him to think I had a jellyfish spine. On the other hand, I didn't want my gravestone to read: CRUSHED BY A YANKEE POND.

"You go ahead. I'll watch," I said.

He positioned himself in the middle of Water Street directly under the shed-sized block of ice. Wagons and carriages made their way around him. A man pushed a handcart over the gutter and up onto the wharf to get out of his way. Lewis didn't seem to notice and kept his face turned upward, waiting.

Overhead, pulleys and cables creaked and groaned as big-muscled men guided the massive block two stories above the street. I held my breath as I watched the ice bounce and sway in midair. The ropes attached to both sides of the block did little to steady it.

"One!" Lewis shouted, and, after a few moments, "two!"—letting me know each time an icy drop plopped down on him.

A mule-drawn wagon clattered over the cobbles. The driver yelled for Lewis to get out of the way. Just at that moment, a drift of sawdust and straw from the ice block above landed on Lewis's head. He started dancing about and waving his hands, as if attacked by hornets. Spooked, the mule bolted forward into traffic, barely missing Lewis. Carts lurched; people scattered. A white sailor crashed into a vegetable stall, causing a pyramid of potatoes to collapse and roll into the street. The vendor screeched and flapped her arms at Lewis like a riled-up chicken.

"Let's get out of here," Lewis said, and shot off through the crowd, running as fast as he could. I followed, walking at normal speed, and found him panting on a thick coil of rope by the dock's edge.

"You look like you've been rolling in a barn," I said, laughing.

"Do I?" He brushed his face and hair to get rid of the sawdust and hay.

I saw Johnny Dancy on his bicycle, coming toward us. He was the last person I wanted to run into. I slipped behind a barrel of turpentine, hoping he wouldn't see me, but no such luck.

He stopped his bicycle next to Lewis. "I been looking all up and down the wharf for you. Let's go."

"Where are we going?" I said.

Lewis and Johnny looked at each other.

"I'm going with Johnny." Lewis swallowed hard.

"Oh," I said, and waited.

"Where?" I finally said.

"Mr. Dancy's taking us aboard a schooner."

As collector of customs, Johnny's father had access to the ships. I loved schooners. Lewis didn't even like them that much.

I looked at Lewis. He looked at Johnny. There was an awkward pause.

"What about the kite?" I said lamely, as if a kite could compete with a giant vessel with four masts taller than most trees.

"We'll do that tomorrow," Lewis said.

Johnny took out his pocket watch—even Lewis didn't own a pocket watch—and said, "We can't be late."

"See you," I said. "Schooner or later." No one laughed. If only the spaces between the cobbles could slurp me up and make me disappear.

Lewis hopped on the crossbar of Johnny's bike, and they rode toward the Customs House.

I continued along the wharf, where the towering ships were docked, their place of origin painted on the hull: Le Havre, France; Reval, Russia; Bremen, Germany; Liverpool, England. From our port, goods were shipped all over the world.

I wondered which of these boats Johnny and Lewis were going to visit. They would probably even get to meet the skipper.

I felt numb. How come Lewis got to go aboard one of these ships and not me? I kicked a cockleshell along the wooden slats. When I caught up to it, I kicked it again, following the shell along the dock.

It wasn't fair. Johnny had decided he didn't like me, and he didn't even know me. I gave the shell a final boot and it landed next to a fishhook. I put the barbed hook in the shell and took it with me to the Customs House, a few blocks farther along on Water Street.

I found Johnny's bicycle leaning against a palm tree. When I was sure no one was looking, I pressed the fishhook into his front tire until I heard a hissing sound, then I ran away. Let him walk back. If his father was so important, let him call President McKinley for help nabbing the culprit. They would never catch me.

But walking home, I felt my spirits sink lower and lower. Once done, the deed could not be undone. There was no way to rid myself of the knowledge that I had a heart blacker than Blackbeard's.

Every week during the summer, I checked out books from the library at the Masonic Lodge at Eighth and Princess. In the early mornings, before the heat and skeeters got unbearable, I spent several hours reading aloud to Boo Nanny while she boiled clothes in the iron kettle over the fire pit. Her favorite story was *Treasure Island*, the one book I owned. "That Jim's got some starch," she said. "A colored boy needs himself some starch, too, all the things that be thrown his way." She wanted to listen to *Treasure Island* twice, but I convinced her to move on to another adventure story, since I had already read the novel several times and knew Jim's escapades by heart.

I wanted to be like Jim—clever, adventurous, and brave. For a while, when faced with a new situation, I asked myself: What would Jim Hawkins do? But I was too lily-livered.

In one way, I was like Jim: I was clever. Or at least, that was what Daddy told me. He claimed that my high forehead was a sign of intelligence—all that room meant a big brain. I thought I looked funny, more like a pint-sized old man starting to lose his hair.

Daddy was the smartest person I knew, even smarter

than Miss Annie, my fifth-grade teacher. He knew so many big words. In the summer, he made me keep a list of vocabulary words from the novels I read, and then quizzed me on them at the supper table. He called them challenge words. Daddy said I had to have a big vocabulary and good grammar if I wanted to go to Howard University, like he did.

"What about Boo Nanny?" I asked. She didn't know many words, but her words were so colorful and she told such good yarns that I knew you didn't need a big vocabulary to get your point across.

"Your grandmother hasn't had the advantages you have. It was against the law for slaves to learn to read and write. But you—you have a bright future. There's no limit to opportunity, if you learn to speak proper English."

I learned not to use big words around Boo Nanny. The trick was to modify your language depending on who you were around. That was one of my challenge words: *modify*.

Once, I corrected Boo Nanny's grammar, and I never did that again. She asked me to go fetch some wood, then said, "I would of went and got it myself, but I be tired to the bone." Without thinking, I said, "Would have gone." She rose out of her chair, and she was so mad that I thought for a minute her back was going to straighten itself all the way up, but it stopped at its usual spot. She wagged her finger at me and said, "I speaks the way what I done my whole life, and it's served me just fine up till now. So don't go putting right my words. I be perfectly able to get what I want across, no problem 'tall."

Boo Nanny felt left out when Daddy and I sparred at the supper table, trying to trip up each other with challenge words.

"Summer's time to be free and easy. No need to lay homework on the boy's doorstep. He's got time aplenty to work, and only a few short years to play," she said one evening at supper. I didn't consider the vocabulary game as work, but I didn't want Boo Nanny to feel bad, so I kept quiet.

"Moses loves to read, and it's a great chance for him to learn new words," Daddy said.

"Now you take that Jim fella in *Treasure Island*," Boo Nanny said. "That boy's got a world of common sense. He ain't sitting in the ship's cabin studying a mess of words."

"Are you denigrating education?" Daddy said.

Mama muttered, "Uh-oh," under her breath.

"Don't go talking at me with books in your jaws," Boo Nanny said, wagging her fork at Daddy. "Say what you mean, plain and simple."

I looked at Mama with pleading eyes. She was the only one who could keep the peace when Daddy and Boo Nanny were at cross-purposes. But she had come home from Colonel Gilchrist's too dog-tired to do much.

"You don't approve of continuing Moses's education when he's not in school?" Daddy said.

I didn't like to be the source of a squabble.

"If I had me some cash money, I'd start a school of common sense, 'cause that's what so many needs and so few gots. And you'd be my first pupil," Boo Nanny said to Daddy. "'Cause if it ain't in a book, you don't believe it. The boy needs to learn by living, is all I'm saying."

"Whoa, you two. Ain't nobody here about 'den-eye-grating' book learning," Mama said, stepping in at last. "Ain't no reason in the world he can't learn by living *and* book learning. You both be right."

But that didn't solve the quarrel. Boo Nanny jerked the dishes about loudly as she cleared the table, and Daddy skulked away to the parlor, leaving me feeling low.

In the heat of summer, Boo Nanny wore a cabbage leaf on her head when she worked outside stirring a boiling pot of laundry or hanging out clothes. "Sun can't work its way through," she said. "Never boils your brains out if you wear a cabbage leaf." Because of its cupped shape, the green leaf stayed on her head, even though she was bent.

But inside, when she fired up the woodstove to warm the irons, there was no protection from the heat. It bore down like the hot compresses she put on my brow when I was sick. She had a grim set to her mouth as she worked, and she regularly mopped her face to keep the sweat from dripping onto the clean ironing. She never sang like she did in cooler weather.

"The thing 'bout rich folks is, the hotter the weather, the more laundry they give me. So I ain't complaining, Cocoa Baby," she said.

She called me Cocoa Baby, not Moses, because when I was a little baby, she added laundry starch to my bathwater to make my skin soft, and after it dried, it left a whitish powder that, against my brown skin, looked like powdered cocoa.

While I was watching her iron one day near the end of May, an idea came to me: ice. That was what she needed. If Boo Nanny could hold a cold chunk of ice against her skin when she took a break from ironing, it would cool her right down and make her job more bearable.

We couldn't afford an icebox, so I decided to make my own. It wouldn't have fancy brass handles, oak doors, and a zinc interior like Lewis's icebox from Sears

& Roebuck. Rather, it would be more like the icehouse by the docks, where thick brick walls and sawdust kept the blocks from melting.

I combed the neighborhood for loose bricks and used them to line an old crate that we used to store kindling. Then Lewis gave me a ride on the crossbar of his bike to the sawmill on the edge of town, where a sawdust mound rose higher than a house.

We horsed around for a while and played King of the Mountain—guess who was king?—then did somersaults on the pile. No one could hear our whoops over the loud whine of the circular saw, which ripped into the huge pine trees that workers pushed into it, sending arcs of sawdust spraying everywhere.

When we were tired of playing, Lewis rode off on his bike and I filled a pillowcase with sawdust and carried it home on my back.

There was no call for the iceman to come to where I lived in Darktown, but he visited Lewis's neighborhood three times a week. A card in the front window indicated who wanted ice—yellow for twenty-five pounds, red for fifty, and blue for seventy-five. After I completed my icebox, I went to Lewis's house. As we played marbles, I listened for the tinkle of the bell that announced the arrival of Mr. Willis's ice wagon.

Mr. Willis had light brown hair, blue eyes, and huge

arms like the men who moved cotton on the wharf. He was a nice man and always let us pet his gray horse, Josie. When he pulled up in front of Lewis's house, he opened the back of the wagon and rearranged the blocks with a huge pair of tongs. When he found the one he wanted, he split it with a hammer and pick, sending a rainbow of silvery slivers flying from the back of the wagon. He covered the split half with sackcloth, hoisted it onto the shoulder of his leather vest, and carried it to the icebox on Lewis's back porch. While he waited for payment, I approached him and asked if he would give me any left-over blocks of ice at the end of the day.

"Sorry, sonny, but that's against company policy. You want ice, that'll be cash on the barrelhead." The sackcloth on his shoulder dripped onto the sand.

I explained in detail how I had made an icebox out of bricks and sawdust for Boo Nanny. I was careful to call her Grandmother and not Boo Nanny, for fear a white person would find the name queer.

"You're a clever boy," Mr. Willis said.

"I'm not asking for a handout," I said. "I'll help you on your route." He pocketed the money from Lewis's maid and went back to his wagon.

"Well, I reckon there's nothing anywhere in the regulations against bartering," he said.

He gave me a twenty-five-pound block of ice that

very day. "That should last you three days, if you did a good job constructing your box," he said. "You let me know how that works out and we'll call it even." He whistled, and his horse moved forward.

I wrapped the ice in a burlap sack and carried it back in a wheelbarrow I borrowed from Lewis.

At home, Boo Nanny was at the ironing board. I chipped off several pieces and showed her how to rub the ice along her arms and let it melt on her skin.

She hugged me and said, "Cocoa Baby, this be the best present a body could want."

When I left to take the wheelbarrow back to Lewis, she was singing.

Daddy and I needed a place to hide some money. I suggested the woodshed, but Daddy said no, a thief might find it. Finally we decided on the dictionary in the parlor. It dated from his college days. The front and back cover were no longer attached, and the spine was missing entirely, exposing the raveled, stringy burlap back and golden globs of glue.

"Jackson, I don't wants that dog-eared thing messing up my parlor," Mama had said several years before. She liked nice things and worked long hours to earn extra money to buy them. I didn't give a fig about the machine-made carpet or the curio cabinet or the horsehair sofa, which felt stiff and scratchy, like riding bareback buck naked. If I had a choice, I'd rather Mama worked less and was home more.

"We need the dictionary out in the open, where we can get to it easily," Daddy had said.

They argued for a while, but Daddy won out. Mama never went near the dictionary. That made it the perfect place to hide money from her.

Daddy was saving up to buy her a pump organ. The previous summer he had included me in the secret plan. If we went without extras, he said, he could set aside two dollars every week, and a year later, we would have enough money to buy a pump organ.

Every week, Daddy gave me two one-dollar bills, and I put them in the dictionary, starting with the letter A so I could keep track. There were twenty-six letters in the alphabet and fifty-two weeks in a year, so at two weeks per letter, by the time we reached Z, we'd have enough money.

Mama loved music. She always sang around the house. When I was younger, she sang me to sleep with a lullaby:

Close yo' little eyes up, honey,
Purty eyes so warm and sunny.
Fold yo' tiny hands and cross 'um.
Hi, dar, yo's a-playing possum.

Mama had never taken formal music lessons, but she had taught herself to play by ear. Daddy was determined that she would have her own organ.

A year is a long time to keep a secret. Just a month before, we had almost got caught out. We were all in the parlor when Mama walked through, dressed in her Sunday red dress with a satin rose at the waist. She was the prettiest lady in the neighborhood. Everybody said so. She had wavy hair, a thin nose, and skin so light she could pass for a white person. That night, she announced that she was on her way to a debate at the Benjamin Banneker Literary and Library Association. The topic was "Resolved: That Alfred Dreyfus was unjustly convicted of treason," with J. C. Reaves arguing the affirmative and George Carnes on the negative.

Boo Nanny said, "You is dead tired, chile, and you wants to go spending your free time filling up your mind with useless piddle just to please you man? What you needs is not refinement. What you needs is a good night's sleep."

"Mama, I wants to improve myself." Mama's grammar was not up to Daddy's high standards, though he never mentioned it.

"Does you even know what treason is?" Boo Nanny said, setting her crochet work in her lap.

"I reckon I can look it up, same like everyone else."

Mama headed for the dictionary, and Daddy and I both lurched out of our seats.

Daddy was quicker than me and took her up in his arms and moved her away from the dictionary. "Remember the cakewalk? The first time we went out?" He held Mama's hand shoulder high and started prancing.

"You is taken leave of you senses," Boo Nanny said.

"Lord, I don't remember. Only thing I remembers is how I rubbed myself from head to toe with lemon juice to get rid of that smell," Mama said.

"What smell?" I asked, keeping an eye on the dictionary, but she had forgotten all about it.

"That fishy smell," she said.

"I first met your mother when she was working as a sounder. She came to my door and sang a little ditty. How did it go? 'Sadie, Sadie, the seafood lady.'" His voice cracked as he sang.

Boo Nanny made a face. Music was not one of Daddy's gifts.

He continued: "I didn't know which was finer, her voice, her figure, or her face. I bought so many clams and oysters that first time, I was up all night throwing up."

"Why, Jack Thomas, you never told me that," she said with a hand on her hip.

"I didn't want you thinking I was a sickly man. Now let's dance."

"You gone make me late for the debate." She playfully shooed him off and left.

This close call came when we had reached the *V*s. After Boo Nanny left the room, Daddy said there were only a few weeks left until we would get to the end of the alphabet, so we might as well keep our hiding place.

Shortly after school let out in mid-May, I held the dictionary upside down and shook hard. Dozens of dollar bills fluttered onto the carpet. I fanned the book's edges and more money rained down, until there was a large pile, which I divided into stacks and counted. We were two dollars short. I located one of the missing bills, stuck in the dictionary pages, but Daddy said not to worry about the other one. That Saturday, we went to a clock-repair store on Front Street that had advertised an organ for sale for a hundred dollars.

The owner, a small man with a light brown mustache, also repaired organs. Someone who moved West had left this one behind. When Daddy inquired about it, the man removed the magnifying loupe from his eye and put it on his forehead, where it was held by an elastic band. "You don't want this organ," he said. The loupe over his eyebrow looked like a giant pimple.

"Does it work?" Daddy said.

The man ignored him, pulled the loupe back into

place over his eye, and leaned over the watch he had taken apart.

"I said, does the organ work?" Daddy repeated.

"I accept cash only, no down payments," the man said, not looking up from his work.

"I won't know if the terms are agreeable until I see the organ," Daddy said.

"You'll have to move it yourself. My people don't deliver to colored," the man said.

Daddy leaned his arm on the counter and said, "What ward are you in? Do you know John Darnton? I believe he's your alderman. We're on the board together."

The man removed the loupe from his eye. "I bet you're one of those Fusion fellows."

"Actually, I'm a Republican, but we banded together with the Populists to defeat the Democrats in the legislature last year and put in a Fusion governor," Daddy said.

"Well, I reckon that explains why there's so many coloreds in office. Payback."

My mind wandered as they talked about politics, but just when I was getting seriously bored, the owner took us to a back room.

My eyes widened when I saw the organ. Made of mahogany, it was covered with so many spindles, columns, and carvings that it made the fanciest gingerbread houses in Wilmington look plain by comparison. Two round wooden candleholders pivoted out from either side of the keyboard. A row of pull stops changed the tone of the organ to chimes, flutes, and other sounds. I couldn't believe we might have something this nice in our house.

"We'll take it," Daddy said. He didn't bargain, but offered full price.

Daddy pulled out the stack of one-dollar bills and counted them, each one as crisp and flat as if Boo Nanny had ironed it.

He got two newspaper deliverymen with a wagon to move the organ into our parlor, and we waited for Mama to come home from work. She chose this day, of all days, to be late. Daddy paced in the kitchen. He couldn't settle down enough to read the paper as he usually did.

Boo Nanny was fixing dinner when Mama came in, and we all fell silent. She looked at us suspiciously. Daddy asked her to get his jacket from the front porch, hoping she would notice the organ. She walked straight through the parlor and out the front door, and returned with the jacket.

"What you be looking so sheepish for?" she asked Daddy.

"Go back to the parlor. There's something there for you," he said.

When she returned to the parlor, she let out a screech, as if she had just discovered a dead body. We crowded around her as she removed her hands from her mouth and traced the ivory keys, the pull stops, and the carved music stand with her fingertips.

"Why, Jack Thomas, you take the cake," she said.

"Don't be standing there with you mouth gaping open. Play us a hymn," Boo Nanny said.

And she did.

At the beginning of the summer, Lewis and I swam naked in the Cape Fear River, until the town passed an ordinance against it. Some ladies on a riverboat excursion had seen a group of Negro boys skinny-dipping and complained. I knew if I got caught, there'd be a five-dollar fine and a serious licking from Daddy, who, as a member of the Board of Aldermen, had voted in favor of the ordinance.

So instead, we went to a swimming hole I knew about. I made Lewis swear he wouldn't tell anyone about the location, particularly not that stuck-up Johnny Dancy. The only other people who knew about the hole were four white boys around our age. If they got there first, we'd tie their clothes in knots so they couldn't get them apart when they got out. If we were there first, they'd do the same thing to us. It was all in good fun. Though we never spoke, we had a friendly rivalry going on, and both sides seemed to enjoy it.

Honeysuckle grew wild and sweet at the base of a huge oak tree that spread its branches over the swimming hole. Someone had taken a thick rope, the kind used to secure tugboats to the docks, and tied it to a branch. Boards nailed to the trunk formed a ladder to a platform. From there, we would swing out over the water, feet wrapped around the knot at the end of the rope, and then drop into the cool, clear water. Lewis and I spent many hours whooping and hollering, seeing who could swing the highest or make the biggest splash, or who could hold his breath underwater the longest.

One day I saw, underneath the platform, a red cloth tied at four ends and left in the crook of the tree. On my stomach, I reached under the platform, retrieved the bundle, and unwrapped it. Inside was a large cone from a longleaf pine. The stiff brown petals had razor-sharp edges. On a lark, I took the pinecone and replaced it with a cocoon I found attached to a branch.

Three days later, when we went to our swimming spot, the red cloth was still in the crook of the tree. Now it held a robin's egg. The fragile sky-blue egg fit perfectly in my palm. I climbed down the ladder with one hand, cupping the treasure in my other hand.

I returned to my pile of clothes and wrapped the egg in my shirt to protect it. Nearby I found a pretty rock and put it inside the cloth in the secret hiding place in the tree.

From then on, each time I went to the swimming hole, I took along a treasure I had collected—a bird's nest, an unusual seedpod, an insect carcass. I even gave up the conch egg case I had found on the beach with Boo Nanny. The golden series of linked disks, each the size of a threepenny stack, formed a paper-like chain that resembled a mermaid's necklace. Inside some chambers were tiny conchs, small enough to require a magnifying glass to see. Other chambers had a nail-head-sized hole where the baby conchs had escaped, to grow into larger conchs on the ocean floor. I knew my friend would like the conch case as much as I did.

For a couple of weeks, it went like that. I would leave little gifts and find, in return, a surprise. Once I left a pair of shoelaces that I had used to test a dye Boo Nanny made from the barberry bush. The laces came out bright orange instead of the rust brown she had expected, so she rejected the dye lot for her dress material. "I ain't switching my fanny round the backyard looking like no pumpkin," she said.

The shoelaces disappeared from the hiding place in the crook of the tree, and in their stead, my secret friend left a pirate's doubloon, made by placing a penny on a railroad track.

One afternoon we happened upon the white boys swimming. Now there were only three. I broke the un-spoken rule of our rivalry and approached them.

"Where's the other boy?" I asked the redhead who was treading water in the center of the hole. I thought of him as Barberry, after the bush that had turned my shoe-laces orange. The color of his hair was unnatural, even for a white boy.

"He died," Barberry said. "It was his brother." He nodded to the gangly boy whose pale skin looked blue underwater. I had nicknamed him Heron, because he re-minded me of the blue heron with the long neck and skinny legs that lived in the marshes.

I paused and let this sink in. I'd never thought of death as something that happened to white people.

"What of?" I asked.

"Smallpox," Barberry said.

I had heard about the epidemic. When the city tried to put a pesthouse around the corner from my house to quarantine the victims, the neighbors rioted and burned it.

"I'm sorry," I said.

"Why are you sorry? You didn't even know him," Heron said.

"Okay, he ain't sorry," Lewis broke in. Then, asserting his authority, he said, "This is our swimming hole. Now beat it."

The white boys scrambled up the bank, gathered their clothes to their chests, and ran away through the brush, their bare bottoms shining like pale moons. We never saw them there again.

Over the next few days, I kept checking the crook of the tree, hoping that someone would have taken the olive shell I left in the red kerchief and replaced it with a surprise. But no one ever did. I would never know if the secret sharer was the brother who died or one of the other boys. Either way, it made me sad.

THREE

At the end of May, a large tent went up on the corner of Red Cross and Sixth, with banners that announced:

MILLIE—CHRISTINE:
THE TWO—HEADED NIGHTINGALE.
EIGHTH WONDER OF THE WORLD.
THE MOST REMARKABLE HUMAN BEING,
NOW 47 YEARS OF AGE,
EVER BORN TO LIVE.
TWO DAYS ONLY.

Crowds gathered to look at the colorful canvas drawings of the Negro Siamese twins with two heads, four arms, and one body. Lewis and I stood in front of the posters. It cost ten cents to view Millie-Christine, twenty-five cents for the recital.

I had never heard of anything so bizarre, not even Boo Nanny's ghouls and ogres and hideous beings with the head of a man and the body of a wildcat. But those creatures were make-believe. This was a living, breathing human being.

"Is this for real? I can't wait to see it," Lewis said. "Johnny will want to go for sure."

"I do, too," I said, acting as if he meant to include me.

"Where are you going to get the money?"

So what if my father wasn't the collector of customs for the Port of Wilmington. I wasn't going to be left out because of a measly dime. When I mentioned to Mama at supper that I wanted to see Millie-Christine, she said, "I want to go with you."

I was shocked. "Why would you want to see her?" I said.

"Honey baby, they's two people, just like you and me, 'cept they's joined at the small of the back," Mama said. "I be wanting to see them my whole life."

I couldn't believe how much she knew about them. They were famous around these parts, Mama said. Born into slavery in Columbus County, just west of Wilmington, the twins were bought and sold several times, then kidnapped and taken to England by the time they were three. After a trial in London, they were returned to the white family who last owned them.

This family continued to manage their careers after they were freed from slavery. Trained in music and voice, the twins wrote poetry, sewed their own costumes, and spoke five languages.

I had heard sailors on the wharf speaking different languages, but I couldn't conceive of how much intelligence it would take to learn five languages. I was having trouble learning one to Daddy's satisfaction.

"I'm working on an article about the Carolina Twins for Friday's paper," Daddy offered.

"Did you meet them?" Mama said, her eyes bright. "What was they like? Tell me every last thing. I want to hear it all."

"They haven't arrived in town yet, but I interviewed people who knew them. When they were younger, they were the toast of Europe, and wealthy aristocrats arranged salons to hear them sing and recite poetry. They even gave a private recital for Queen Victoria. She was so taken with them that she gave them diamond hair clips."

"Day I spend my hard-earned cash money on the likes of colored freaks be the day you can shovel me under," Boo Nanny said as she cleared the supper dishes.

"Mama, you should be proud. Two people of our race, born in the county right next to us. Imagine, moving from slavery to the salons of Europe."

Boo Nanny snorted. "One of our own gots two heads and four feet, then white folk can't get enough of them. The two-legged kind, they fine and dandy to do without."

"Mama, they ain't freaks. They're talented musicians. They took piano and voice lessons. I always wondered what it'd be like if I'd been trained. I can't read a lick of music."

"We was possum poor when I was raisin' you up. I ain't had myself no extrees for the likes of lessons," Boo Nanny said. The plates rattled against each other as she set them down with a jolt.

"I know, Mama. I'm not complaining. I just wonder how much better I could be with lessons."

"Chile, you got the true gift inside you. You sing better'n those two. More natural-like. Them Carolina Twins is slicker than a bucket of boiled okra," Boo Nanny said.

"Sadie, I didn't know you wanted to take music lessons," Daddy said. "Maybe we can arrange something." Mama was surprising all of us tonight.

"I still says they's freaks. Next thing you know, you's gone tell me a talking mule is pure-t natural."

"Millie-Christine earned enough money in Europe to buy the very plantation over near Whiteville where they were born into slavery. I guess you could call that freakish. They gave the Big House to their parents as a gift, then built a fourteen-room Victorian house on part of the land and retired there," Daddy said.

"That be the God's truth? Well, I never," Boo Nanny said. "In that case, I wants to clap my own two eyes on them."

But when the night of the recital arrived, Boo Nanny claimed to be bone-tired and Daddy begged off, so it was just Mama and me.

She dressed up in her finest dress of blue silk and white lace and looked as stylish as the ladies in the Sears & Roebuck catalog. Mama had a flair for fashion and always added something extra to the dresses she made— a sash, a ruffle, some trim—that made her stand out. She liked to be noticed, except when she went to work in a shapeless dress with a rag on her head.

We got to the tent a little late and stood in the back with the other Negroes. From there, I could easily see over the seated crowd. The stage was lit by torches and held two upright pianos set at an angle, with a single bench forming the crossbar of the letter A. I could feel Mama's excitement. She clutched my arm as the Carolina Twins came onto the stage to great applause. They wore white elbow-length kid gloves and a sleeveless gown of green silk. The dress had two waists with sashes but a single skirt, with a continuous line of ruffles around the bottom, ending halfway down the calf, shorter than what was considered modest for any but the youngest girls. Beneath the single skirt were two pairs of bronze high-top boots.

The twins stood sideways, their shoulders almost touching. One was slightly larger than the other. In their hair, they wore sparkling barrettes. I wondered if these were the diamond hair clips Queen Victoria had given them. I had never before seen diamonds. Of course, neither had I seen someone who had met the Queen of England, nor someone with two heads.

Seeing Millie-Christine in person, I felt a stab of disappointment. I was expecting something more grotesque. They looked so normal. These women could easily be my aunts, only they were better dressed. Had we been hoodwinked? Maybe they weren't connected at all, and that single skirt was a hoax.

But as they walked back to the pianos, the larger one leaned over to pick up a piece of sheet music that had fallen, and she lifted her sister's feet completely off the floor.

The audience fell silent as they played piano duets. There was no whispering or fidgeting or coughing. People gave the music their full attention.

As the twins played, I stared at their backs, and my mind went to strange places as I tried to picture how they were connected. Did they have two bottoms or one? Did they use a double-seater privy? When one had a toothache, did the other? If you tickled the foot of one, would the other giggle? I didn't even listen to the piano playing.

I wondered what it must be like for her, or them—I still didn't know how to think about this double person—to be stared at their whole lives. I couldn't imagine anything worse. I tried my best not to be noticed at all times.

As part of the program, the twins recited poems in French, German, and Italian, trading off verses. But my favorite was a poem they had written themselves:

> Two heads, four arms, four feet,
> All in one perfect body meet;
> I am most wonderfully made,
> All scientific men have said.
>
> I am happy, quite, because I'm good;
> I love my Savior and my God;
> I love all things that God has done,
> Whether I'm created *two* or *one*.

By the time they began singing in close harmony, I had stopped thinking about their oddity and started enjoying the recital. They had beautiful voices. Millie, the smaller one, sang alto, and Christine sang soprano.

I glanced over at Mama. Her lips slightly apart, her head leaning forward a little, she was completely engaged.

By the middle of "Jeanie with the Light Brown Hair," Mama had tears rolling down her nose and dripping onto her chin. Mama was tough and never cried, not even when grease jumped from the fry pan to her arm and made the skin bubble up and peel back to reveal the pink underneath. It unsettled me to see her weeping.

"Beautiful," she whispered as the tent broke out into loud applause. "If only I could sing like that." She dabbed her eyes with a handkerchief.

The united twins ended the evening with a polka. I was reminded of the races at Sunday school picnics where you link arms with someone back to back and run to the finish line, one person leading with the right leg and the other with the left. Unlike those comical and awkward races, the Two-Headed Nightingale danced in perfect harmony, performing the steps in unison and in time to the music.

The crowd rose to its feet when they finished. I had to stand on my tiptoes to see the twins curtsy, making a graceful sweep with their back arms while holding hands with their front two arms. Mama was the last one to stop clapping.

Afterward, the Carolina Twins moved crablike down the center aisle in an expanding V, signing autographs on opposite sides. Most performers would have ignored the small group of Negroes in the back, but they made a special effort and warmly greeted the people of our race.

When the attached ladies reached us, I thought Mama was going to faint, she was so nervous. To my surprise, she spoke up, her voice scratchy. "Your voices is so lovely. You touched my soul."

"Why, *merci*," one of the twins said.

"That is so kind of you," said the other, and took extra time to sign Mama's program.

When we got home, I looked at what she had written: "A soul with two thoughts. Two hearts that beat as one. With Millie Chrissie's love."

Mama took the program and put it in a special box in the parlor. "This be a treasure always," she said, and sat down to play the organ.

Every May 30, the Negroes celebrated National Memorial Day at the federal cemetery off Market Street. White folks hated the place. They called it the Union cemetery. As far as they were concerned, it was full of Union traitors, carpetbaggers, coloreds, and Yankee lovers—a toss-up as to which was worse. White people celebrated Confederate Memorial Day on May 10 at Oakdale Cemetery, where their family members were buried. But for the black citizens of Wilmington, National Memorial Day was an important holiday.

This year my daddy, as a member of the Board of Aldermen, was selected to be the keynote speaker. Johnny's father may have been the most important Negro in Wilmington, and Lewis's father the richest, but mine was the smartest. I was excited about hearing his speech.

The afternoon of the celebration, I was at Lewis's house messing around in the attic and the time slipped away. When I checked the clock, I saw I had only fifteen minutes before Daddy was scheduled to speak, and the cemetery was a couple of miles away. Lewis let me borrow his bike.

I pedaled as fast as I could and arrived at the federal cemetery with time to spare. I left the bike by one of the identical white headstones that stretched out in long rows, rising and falling with the lay of the land.

I made my way through the noisy crowd that filled the open field. People had spread out plates and food on quilts. Children in their Sunday best ate the last of the strawberry crop or sucked peppermint candy sticks that turned their lips red. Some prankish boys slipped firecrackers into the huge pit beneath the roasting pig and laughed when the adults jumped as the firecrackers popped off.

People had gathered to celebrate the soldiers who died in the War Between the States. Truth be told, I didn't know much about the war. When I was younger, Lewis and I played war with sticks for weapons and magnolia pods for artillery. Lewis played the part of the victorious Union Army and made me take the Confederate side.

I knew the Rebels were bad men. That was why Lewis made me play them. But I was surprised at Boo Nanny's fury when I told her about it.

"Honey chile, you gone stark raving mad, playing a Rebbie boy?"

"But Lewis made me."

"Can't nobody make you do nothing, lessen you let them," she had said.

Now I searched the crowds for Boo Nanny and Mama, but before I could find them, Daddy mounted the stage, which was covered with flags and red, white, and blue bunting. The band stopped playing. Mothers shushed their children, and everyone looked in Daddy's direction. He was a slight man, not grand and imposing like some of the preachers in town. But he had a booming voice and could easily be heard without using a speaking trumpet.

When everyone was quiet, he began by thanking various people for making the event possible. My mind wandered, and when I came out of my daydreaming, he was already into his speech.

"Ten percent of the Union Army was composed of our Negro brethren. Some were runaway slaves; some were freedmen. Some lived, and too many died."

He was quiet for a moment, and the crowd followed him in silence. You could hear the rustle of leaves and a bird's call.

"The headstones to your right commemorate the United States Colored Troops who died in the battles of Sugar Loaf and Forks Road. There are also cooks, teamsters, and other colored U.S. Army personnel buried there."

Lined up like soldiers, the headstones sparkled pure white under the afternoon sun. I could not tell where the graves of the colored soldiers left off and the white section began.

"These brave men sacrificed so that we could become family members, productive citizens, and home owners. It is their sacrifice that we honor today."

There was scattered applause.

"These soldiers could not have imagined a city like Wilmington, where, two years shy of the twentieth century, people of color would hold four of the ten seats on the Board of Aldermen. Where thirteen of the twenty-four policemen would be black. Where fourteen percent of Negroes would own their own homes, in a community with lawyers and doctors of color and a solid middle class. These achievements are beyond the wildest dreams of the soldiers resting beneath these rows of headstones. And yet, none of this—none of it—would be possible without their sacrifice.

"The twentieth century promises to be a century of opportunity for our race. If we continue to work to better ourselves, we can scale Olympic heights so that these soldiers' lives will not have been spent in vain."

At the end of his speech, people jumped to their feet, shouted, and waved their hands. When the cheering died down, the band struck up.

I felt myself swell like a bullfrog's throat. I didn't understand everything Daddy said, but I understood that he was someone people looked up to, and that made me proud.

I went to find him, but he was surrounded by wellwishers, so I decided to return Lewis's bike and walk home.

The bike was not where I thought I'd left it. The white headstones stretched out in identical rows. It wasn't hard to confuse one row with another. I walked up and down every row looking for Lewis's bright blue bike. As I got closer to the stone wall where the graves ended, my heart started thumping. The crowd was breaking up, and I came to the conclusion that I should have reached earlier but had dared not consider: someone had stolen Lewis's bike.

My stomach felt as if I had eaten bad oysters. Lewis was my best friend. But when he found out that I had lost his bike, he would chuck me for good.

Trudging along the roadside in the sand, I tried to think of what to tell him. The only solution I could come up with was to buy him another bike. But I had been saving my pennies for months to buy my own wheels, and even after adding my Christmas money, I barely had enough for one wheel, on sale at the hardware store.

I dragged myself up to Lewis's front porch, my body heavier and heavier with each step. The maid answered the door when I knocked. The starched white apron she wore over her long gray skirt made me think of a nurse. She told me that Lewis was out for a carriage ride with his family. I let out a sigh. I had more time. I told her to tell him that I would bring the bike back the next day.

At supper, while Mama and Boo Nanny carried on about Daddy's triumph, I kept quiet. That night I barely slept. The next day, I got up and out of the house early, vowing to scour every block in town until I found the missing bike. I told Boo Nanny that I was walking to the ocean—that would take all day.

"Don't go forgetting my conchs," she said as I went out the door. In the backyard, next to the big iron pot where she boiled the laundry, she had secured a piece of driftwood upright, then placed a conch shell on each of the points of wood. We had an agreement that anytime I went to the shore, I would look for a conch to add to her tree.

I started out on my street, Fifth, which was divided by a median. I walked on the right side, looking into all the backyards. Across the bridge over the railroad tracks, the houses started getting bigger and more ornate. They were painted pastel colors and had large front porches with fancy railings and windows as big as doors. I walked by quickly. It was unlikely that rich people would steal a bike, but still, I checked every backyard, just to be sure. I kept walking on Fifth for about a mile until I got to Dry Pond, where the po-bocra lived. Here, the houses were more like shacks, as small as the houses in my neighborhood but not as neatly kept. The yards were mostly sand, with a few sprigs of grass here and there. Drooping from the enormous oaks along the roadside were hanks of moss—haint's hair—filled with chiggers.

I felt uneasy as I went down the narrow streets, looking into front and backyards. Here I was the only black face, unlike the fancy areas of town, where a few rich Negroes lived and maids walked to and from work.

A man in overalls approached me. He was carrying a copy of the *Wilmington Messenger*, the white newspaper. "Where you headed, boy?"

"I'm just walking," I said.

"You got to be walking somewheres. Where would that be?"

"Down the road," I said.

"Well, you best turn back. You ain't welcome here."

I went up a side street and turned back toward town on a parallel street. Several blocks down, I passed a tar-paper shack surrounded by a peeling white fence with rotted pickets. In the front yard, beside an anchor half buried in the sand, was a bright blue bike lying on its side—Lewis's wheels.

I looked around. It was a hot day and no one was out in the streets. I eyed the mongrel dogs sleeping under the house and calculated the distance between the bike and the front gate. The sand was thick and there was little grass, so I probably wouldn't be able to ride off. I'd have to grab the bike and run until I got to the street, which, in this poor part of town, was packed sand instead of cobblestones.

Before I could chicken out, I climbed over the side fence and snuck up behind a tree. The dogs didn't stir. I darted toward the bike, grabbed the handlebars, and lit out for the street. The dogs scrambled from beneath the house, barking, but I was out the gate before they could reach me. I thought I was home free, when suddenly a huge man shot out the front door like a wad from a spitball gun. "Hey, you! Thief! Stop!" he yelled, running after me.

At the end of the block, the man in overalls who had stopped me earlier appeared out of nowhere. As I pedaled past, he hurled the newspaper at me. It hit me in the face, and the bike slid on the slippery brown pine needles that covered the road. Both men reached me at the same time.

"That kid stole my boy's bike," the big man said.

I was trembling but managed to say, "It's not your son's bike."

"Ain't no nigger tells me what's what."

"Do you want me to go fetch the law?" the man in overalls said. In this part of town there were no telephones.

"Forget it. I'll take care of him right now."

He grabbed me by the shirt and a button popped off. I braced for the worst.

"Let him go," the man in overalls said. "He's not a bad boy. He's learned his lesson, and you've got your son's bike now."

"He'll come back and help himself to anything that's not nailed down. That's the way these people are."

While they were arguing, I grabbed the bike and took off. I was all the way down the block before they started running. I darted down a side street, then zigzagged along the city streets until I was sure I had ditched them.

I rode the bike directly to Lewis's house. The maid got him and he came outside. "I brought your bike back," I said.

He looked over my shoulder, down the steep porch steps. Rubbing the crust from his eyes, he said, "That's not my bike."

"Wh-wh-what do you mean?" I was sure he had not fully woken up.

"Mine's a Columbia. That's an Eagle."

I went numb.

"Johnny saw my bike at the celebration and didn't think I'd mind if he took it for a spin. When he returned and couldn't find me, he brought it over to my house. Where the heck did those wheels come from?"

I looked at the stolen bike. I was a thief.

Lewis invited me to stay and play marbles, but I begged off. I needed to figure this out. The obvious thing was to return the bike to the owner, but I was terrified. That man would kill me if he saw me again.

I decided to go to the ocean. I always felt better when I went to the ocean. At least I could turn the lie I told Boo Nanny into the truth. Then I would only be a thief, instead of a liar *and* a thief.

The back road to the beach passed along the edges of

the salt marshes. The tides mixed with freshwater streams to feed the tall grasses and create a vast field of green that, waving in the wind, made me seasick if I looked at it too long. The road ended at the dunes. I walked the bike through the thick sand to the ocean.

The sky was a colorless blue, like the marbles we called aggies. The sun formed a dull halo behind the clouds, but it cast a glaring silver pathway across the sea, like the moon sometimes did.

The waves lapped at the shore, pushing on their forward edge a trim of foam. The wind lifted the froth and sent it skimming over the sand until it broke off into smaller clumps, then disappeared, and another wave brought a new batch. I wanted to ride for miles and miles, with the wind against my face, trying to outrun my troubles.

Being at the beach usually cheered me up, but today the sea was not my friend. Before starting home, I left the bike on its side on the sand and walked along the shore to look for a conch for Boo Nanny's tree. No other people were in sight.

A short distance away, I found a half-buried sand dollar. The flat white disk had a star etched on its face and five slitlike holes. This was a sign. It would fetch me good luck. I slipped the sand dollar into my pocket and walked on.

It took me longer than I thought it would to find a conch, but I was glad I kept looking, because the shell I found was the prettiest yet—tan with streaks of pink and orange.

The bike had no basket, so I put the conch inside my shirt, with the sharp points away from me. On the way back, I took the toll road, since it was shorter and bikes could ride for free. I pedaled along the packed shoulder past mule-drawn wagons and carriages, their metal wheels crunching against the crushed oyster-shell surface.

No one was in our backyard when I stashed the bike behind the shed. Before going into the house, I took out the conch and then reached into my pocket for my good-luck charm. To my horror, I discovered that the sand dollar had broken into pieces. Among the fragments were four tiny chips that looked like doves.

The kitchen was filled with the spicy smell of molasses cookies. One batch was cooling on top of the pie safe. Boo Nanny was rolling out the last of the dough on the kitchen table. She used an empty baking-powder tin as a cookie cutter.

Daddy was at the table by the window reading a book. If he was sitting and not eating, chances were he had his nose in a book.

"Make youself useful and go fetch me a load of wood before you get too comfortable," Boo Nanny said when she saw me at the door. After my miserable day, I couldn't wait to get into the spicy-smelling kitchen, but I went back to the woodpile and brought an armload of split logs to the porch.

"What's the matter, sugar? You had youself a bad day?" Boo Nanny said when I came in the second time.

I gave her the conch, then took out the pieces of the sand dollar and showed them to her.

"I found these inside." I showed her the chips.

"Doves of peace," she said, shaking her head knowingly.

"They're good luck, aren't they?" I said. I couldn't imagine doves of peace being bad luck.

"You be missing one."

I counted four.

"They's five slits in the sand dollar. Two for the nails in sweet Jesus's hands, two for the nails in his feet—and one for the Roman sword. You be missing one. That be a powerful sign you got a mess of trouble coming to your door."

"Josephine, don't go putting nonsense into the boy's head," my father said, looking up from his book.

"I don't hardly 'spect you to believe me, Jack, but I knows what I knows."

Then, as if a signal that the bad luck would start that very moment, Daddy said, "Whose bike is that out back?"

"Huh?" I said, fingering the sharp edges of the broken sand dollar in my pocket.

"The one you put behind the shed."

He must have looked up from his book just as I arrived. I felt searing heat spread across my chest, knowing that Daddy had watched me hide the plunder like some common area sneak.

"It's Lewis's. I mean, I thought it was. I borrowed his bike and then it disappeared and it was all my fault and I felt terrible and I'm not a thief. . . ." Everything came out in a confused rush as I blathered on, not making much sense.

"Whoa. Slow down, son. It's all right. Now tell me, as simply as you can, what happened."

I tried my best. When I finished, he paused a moment to ponder what I had said. "I'm not blaming you. I don't want you to think that," he said slowly. "But you need to return the bike to its rightful owner and apologize. It doesn't matter if you thought you were taking what belonged to you—it's stealing nonetheless."

I remembered that angry white man and shuddered. "Have you been to Dry Pond, Daddy? Those people hate us there."

He took off his glasses and rubbed the bridge of his nose. "That may be true, but that doesn't change anything."

"I bet he's Ku Klux."

"What the man is or isn't has nothing to do with what you are. It's not your bicycle. I'm not blaming you. I'm just saying that you have to set things right."

I thought of what Boo Nanny had said about trouble coming to my door. "But he might kill me."

Daddy seemed indifferent to the possibility, which shocked me. "It's easy for a man to be hateful in a group. It's harder when he's face to face. You'll show him what you're worth. A real man admits his mistakes."

I felt miserable. "But I'm not a man. I'm a boy."

"I'll go with you, if that will make you feel better."

Daddy closed his book and went to the other room. I slumped down at the table.

"You appear to me to be a boy in need of some molasses cookies," Boo Nanny said. "Go grab youself a handful, and don't tell you mama or she'll go accusing me of ruining your supper."

I went to bed early but could not get to sleep. After a while, Mama came into the room. "You playing possum?" she said. The moon filled the curtains with light, but the bed was dark.

I kept my eyes shut and remained still, hoping she would go away.

"You ain't asleep. I know you ain't."

She sat on the edge of the bed and smoothed my forehead. She smelled of lemons. I could hear the clock ticking in the parlor.

"When I was a child, I stole something once," she said.

"You what?" I opened my eyes and sat up. I was shocked. I couldn't believe Mama had ever done anything wrong.

"You knows 'bout how I couldn't get enough of Millie-Christine, the colored Siamese twins." I listened carefully as she described the time when she was fifteen and Millie-Christine came to town. They had just returned from a European tour and were at the height of their fame. Mama couldn't afford to see them, but some of the stores carried their autobiography, *The History of the Carolina Twins, Told in Their Own Peculiar Way by One of Them.* A drawing of the twins was on the cover.

In the store, she slipped the paper pamphlet into the back waistband of her skirt and covered it with her jacket. The clerk smiled at her as she walked out. Back home Boo Nanny found the pamphlet.

"Whoo-ee. You should a seed Boo Nanny. That kind of mad you don't never forget," Mama said in the dark.

Boo Nanny made her return the pamphlet and apologize to the clerk.

"What did you say to him?" I said.

"I don't rightly remember. Only thing I remember was he thought I was a straight-out white gal, and when he found out I was colored, he said, 'You is some kind of purty,' and gave me a long, ugly, adult kind of look. Boo Nanny dragged me out of there quick and said, 'I don't want you ever to get anywheres near that man, you hear? He's no-count.' After that, I never stole another blessed thing."

"Why was he a bad man?" I asked.

"Honey, it don't matter. You too young for that. Important thing is, I done something wrong, and had to make it right."

We sat in the dark, in silence. After a while, I said, "Mama, I'm scared."

"I know, honey, but you be just fine tomorrow."

The next day, I met Daddy at his office near the docks and we walked together to Dry Pond, with me pushing the bike. When I found the house, I looked over the fence. The dogs were not in the yard, so I leaned the bike against the fence inside the gate and went to the porch, praying no one would be home. But the man answered the door. Standing a step above us, he was even larger than I remembered, and he smelled of liquor. I glanced behind him. Empty tins littered the floor, and a sheet was wadded up on a bare mattress. A sour stench came from the room, so different from my house, which was filled with happy smells.

He looked at me, then at Daddy, and chewed the corner of his lip. He didn't recognize me until he saw the bike against the fence.

"What you want?" he growled.

The porch felt wobbly beneath me. I fixed my eyes on my feet and waited without speaking, afraid my voice would crack. Daddy gently poked me in the side. "Go ahead, son."

I looked down and mumbled, "I'm sorry."

Daddy said, "He can't hear that. Look the man in the face and tell him."

I gazed directly into his hard eyes and explained how I had mistaken the bike in his yard for my friend's bike.

"Your son's a liar," the man said.

"My son's not a liar. He's apologizing, which shows character."

"Get off my porch," he said.

I wanted to tell Daddy "I told you so," but he pulled back his shoulders and, without any display of fear, said, "We've done what we came to do. Good day."

FOUR

A sunken train track divided Darktown from Lewis's neighborhood, which was mostly white. A bridge allowed people and carriages to pass over. I knew the schedule of the trains by heart. Our house was only a few blocks away, and I heard the whistles. Grandpa Tip was a porter on the Atlantic Coast Line Railroad, and I took a great interest in trains.

Grandpa Tip was freed by a Quaker lawyer in Jamestown when he was a boy. He went to a Quaker school and learned how to read and cipher. Education was important to him, and he made sure that Daddy went to college. Boo Nanny grew up as a house slave and never learned to read and write. For whatever reason, she didn't get along with Grandpa Tip. I'd heard her tell neighbors that he put on airs, but really I think she was ashamed to be around him because she didn't know how to read.

Grandpa Tip promised to give me and Daddy train tickets for my twelfth birthday in October. I was so excited. Nights, I lay awake listening to the whistle of the locomotive and counting off the weeks.

The banks to the sunken train tracks were steep, but easy to go down if you grabbed the struts of the bridge and lowered yourself by holding on to the woody bushes that clung to the banks. One day in July, Lewis and I were playing in our territory along the tracks. I say our territory because some white boys our age liked to play on the tracks, too. I recognized two of the four from the swimming hole earlier that summer. The redhead I called Barberry was the ringleader. Heron, the one who had lost his brother, was also part of the gang.

The dividing line was the Fifth Street bridge, with the space directly under the bridge designated as neutral territory. No one wanted to stay under the bridge for long, since manure often plopped through the slats when a carriage passed overhead. Weeds grew freely under the bridge, even though the space was in shadow most of the time.

That day, the white boys hurled pebbles at us. "Dare you to come on our side," Barberry said.

They had us, four to two. "No way we're coming over there!" I yelled in answer to the challenge. "Your side's haunted."

"You're fibbing!" Barberry shouted.

"Ask the old-timers. A woman was run over by a train. Right over there." I pointed to a spot deep in their territory. "Her head was sliced off and flipped up into an open cargo car," I said, making up the story as I went along. I had heard enough tales from Boo Nanny to create my own.

The white boys' eyes widened, and they listened closely.

"They say she waits here for the train, hoping to get her head back," I said.

"Was she white or colored?" said Heron. I wanted to feel sorry for him because he lost his brother, but he made it hard.

"It doesn't matter after death. All haints are white," I said, wondering if a colored ghost would be more or less frightening to them.

"I ain't skeert. Ghosts don't come out in the day," Barberry said. For a white boy, he had bad grammar.

"Not usually. But you know how sometimes you can see the moon in the afternoon sky? It's like that," I said.

"I don't believe you," Heron said. He had a few whiskers and his voice had already started to change.

"Fine, then meet Moses at the bridge after dark and wait for the ghost," Lewis said. I shot him a glance. What was he getting me into?

"So you'll wait with us?" Barberry asked me.

"Heck no. That's your side," I said. "I'll watch from the bridge."

"What's the matter? Too skeert?" he said.

"No, too smart. You couldn't pay me to go on your side, not even in broad daylight," I said.

The white boys looked nervously at each other. Heron was the first to back out. Two others made excuses. That left Barberry. He hesitated.

"Go ahead, Tommy. You do it," Heron said, and pushed him toward our side.

So the redhead had a name. *Tommy* didn't suit him as well as *Barberry*.

"Dare you," Lewis said. "You're too scared."

"Am not," said Tommy.

"Are too."

"Not."

"Too."

Lewis put his hands under his armpits and flapped his elbows, going "polk puck puck polk" and thrusting his head forward like a pecking chicken.

After some negotiating, we agreed on a time to meet and sealed the deal with a handshake under the bridge. Both of us quickly hopped back onto our respective sides as a wagon rattled the planks overhead.

Later, after the white boys left, Lewis said, "That ghost story wasn't true, was it?"

"I made it up."

"Shew. You had me fooled for a minute."

We mapped out our plan for the evening and then parted company.

That night at the appointed time, I snuck out my window. I didn't have anything to be scared of, since I had made up the yarn about the ghost, but my stomach felt fluttery nonetheless.

I arrived at the bridge just as a city worker was climbing a ladder to ignite the kerosene streetlamp. Light fell through the slats and striped the neutral territory beneath the bridge.

I didn't expect Tommy to show up, but he did. I offered to go down by the tracks and wait with him.

"You'd do that?" he said.

"Sure." I felt guilty for getting more credit than was my due. I knew there were no ghosts.

Light from the streetlamp allowed us to see our way to the bottom of the steep bank, but its reach ended as we walked along the tracks, deep into Tommy's territory. I had never walked on the white side before, even when the boys were not there to guard it.

We sat by the tracks and waited. It was dark and silent, but for the occasional *clip-clop* of hooves on the bridge and the bobbing light from the carriage lanterns.

"If we talk, it might keep the haints away," I said.

He told me about his two little sisters and his dog, Rusty, who had fur the same color as his hair. He was so lucky. I had always wanted a little brother or sister. Sometimes it got lonely living with adults. I didn't even have a dog.

Tommy didn't seem interested in my family, but when I told him that I was going to ride the train to Fayetteville in October for my twelfth birthday, he said, "Wow. I've never known anyone who's taken the train."

Lewis rode the train all the time, but I didn't want to make Tommy feel bad. His family lived in Dry Pond, the poor neighborhood where I'd snatched the bicycle.

Tommy made me promise that I would remember every detail of the train ride so I could tell him. "If you do that, I'll show you the tunnels under the city."

"The ones used as an escape route for runaway slaves?" I asked.

"No, the ones the Confederate soldiers used to hide from the Union Army," Tommy said.

"You've actually been there?" I said. Wait until Lewis found out about this.

"Yep."

"Deal," I said. We agreed on a time and place to meet the following day. I couldn't believe he would let me in on such a prized secret.

Suddenly Tommy grabbed my shoulder and said, "What's that?"

"I don't hear anything."

"No, listen." We were silent, and from the darkness above there came a moan that sounded like a cross between a hoot owl and a whip-poor-will.

"There. That," Tommy whispered.

"Probably some bird."

The sound continued, and it was indeed spooky.

"There she is!" Tommy yelled. "Up there!"

A white filmy form floated above us, dancing and changing shapes as it descended through the darkness.

Tommy shouted, "Beat it!" and made a beeline for the bridge. I followed.

He was terrified, and I felt lousy about our prank. As planned, Lewis had balled up a sheet and thrown it over the tracks. As it floated down in the dark, the sheet folded in on itself and puffed out again, looking exactly like a ghost.

I caught up to Tommy and watched as he launched himself against the bank, like a fly against glass, then slid down. He was so scared that his limbs didn't work properly. I made a stirrup with my hands and he put a foot in. I hoisted him up and he caught hold of one of the bridge supports and was able to lift himself over the top. When he got there, he gave me a hand and pulled me up the bank.

Then, without a word, he dashed down the road into the dark.

Lewis came out from his hiding spot. "Ha! Did you see that fellow scramble off? Yellow belly!" Lewis said, prancing about as if at a cakewalk.

I didn't like Lewis laughing at him. Truth was, Tommy had been much braver than me, because I knew there was no ghost. "Let's drop it," I said, feeling sour.

"Those boys aren't coming anywhere near our track again, no way," Lewis said, gloating over the success of the caper.

"I don't want to hear any more about it," I said.

"What's your problem? We just won a major victory."

But I felt rotten. I had come to like Tommy, and we had humiliated him with a silly prank. That was no way to treat a friend.

The next morning, Tommy met me at the appointed spot, holding a lantern in broad daylight. Luckily, no people were around. It took both of us to roll off the heavy iron disk covering a shaft that descended like an old well. A rusty ladder was attached to one side. A tube of daylight fell fifteen feet and then ended.

Tommy went down ahead of me to the last rung. "I

can see the bottom. But I need you to hold the lantern while I jump," he said.

I did, and he swung from the bottom rung and easily dropped to the ground. He took the lantern from me, and I jumped.

We found ourselves in a tunnel a little over five feet high. In a couple of years, I wouldn't be able to stand without hunching over, but now I could. The brick ceiling arched overhead. Timbers shored up the sides. In some spots, the walls were brick, and in others, merely dirt, with no visible means of support.

It was low tide, and the brackish water was but a trickle—more like a foul sludge. The ground was covered with rocks, chunks of brick, and broken seashells. The tunnel reeked of fish and night soil.

Tommy led with the lantern, and I followed. Because of the arch of the ceiling, we had to stay toward the center, and I couldn't avoid sloshing in the stream and getting the smelly silt on my shoes.

We came to an area crisscrossed with thousands of silvery lines, giving the walls a strange and beautiful iridescent glow in the lantern light. Looking closer, I saw the source: slugs, leaving their silver traces on the damp walls.

"Do you think there are ghosts down here?" Tommy said.

"I doubt it. They like to be out where they can scare humans," I said, warming to the role Tommy had assigned me as ghost expert. Spirits had a way of leveling out the power between people, and I liked that.

Up ahead, something splashed through the water and streaked into the darkness.

"A rat." I shuddered.

"No, bigger," Tommy said. Spooked, he turned and ran. Before he got too far, he tripped and plunged headfirst into the water, no deeper than a puddle. The lantern slipped from his hand. Glass shattered, and then everything went dark.

I stopped in my tracks and waited a few seconds for my eyes to adjust, but the blackness didn't get any lighter. I held my hand a few inches in front of my nose and couldn't see it. Even on the darkest night with no moon or stars, there was enough light to turn the ocean glossy black. Now I realized that everything I had ever thought of as black was not truly black. This was something altogether different: complete, absolute darkness. Chills spread across my back.

"Tommy, are you all right?"

He didn't say anything.

"Be careful of the glass when you get up," I said.

I held my hands in front of me and moved slowly toward the sniffles.

"Are you crying?" I said.

"No," he blubbered.

"Stay there. I'm coming."

I shuffled forward. My foot got tangled in the handle of the lantern and I stumbled, but I caught myself. Finally my hand hit Tommy's wet shirt. I was right next to him and still couldn't see a thing.

"Grab my hand," I said.

"Yuck."

"Okay, don't." I splashed forward.

"Wait, wait. Don't leave me," Tommy croaked.

I backed up a few steps. "I'm not going to leave you. Here." I took off my belt and pressed one end into his hand. "Loop your finger through the buckle. I'll lead the way."

With one hand holding the belt behind me and my other hand over my head, I steadied myself against the crumbling brick ceiling and sloshed through the soupy muck. My hand touched something gooey. Mud? Slugs? I kept going.

Dragging my feet through the water, I stumbled on something bigger than a conch shell but smaller than a human skull. I kicked it aside and continued.

"What was that?" Tommy said.

"Nothing," I said, trying not to think about what it might have been.

"They'll never find us down here," Tommy blubbered.

"They don't have to. We'll find our own way out," I said confidently.

"How?"

"We can't get lost. It's like a train track. It only goes in one direction," I said. But I felt the underside of my tongue tighten, the way it does before vomiting, when I realized that I could have gotten turned around. What if I was headed in the wrong direction? It was like swimming underwater and getting all confused and not knowing which way was which when you came up for air.

Nobody knew where we were. Nobody. Nobody knew we were together, nor would they ever guess. I felt a sickness wash over me. My legs started to buckle, but I stiffened them. *Stay calm,* I told myself. *Just stay calm.* I took a deep breath and nearly choked on the rank-smelling air.

Soon I reached a place where the ceiling ended. Now when I waved my hand over my head, I felt only emptiness. My feet didn't feel attached to the ground, and I had the sensation of floating. Had I been in this spot before? I tried to remember a place with a raised ceiling, but I hadn't been paying attention. I began to doubt everything. My heart was filled with terror—not the fake thrill of being scared by ghost stories, but a genuine terror. Every step I took could be a step in the wrong direction.

After a short distance, I found the ceiling again and continued. Finally, up ahead, I saw an eyebrow of light. I didn't realize I had been holding so much bad air in my lungs until it came whooshing out. It was the manhole cover. We had left a gap so we could easily remove it. The rusty ladder was visible in the sliver of light.

"We made it!" I cried.

I hoisted Tommy up, and we climbed into a world bleached white. Rolling around in the grass, we giggled with the pure joy of being aboveground.

"Pee-yew. You stink," Tommy said.

"You do, too."

"Let's ditch these clothes and take a dip in the river," Tommy said. We were both covered in mud.

"If they catch us skinny-dipping, we'll get a fine," I said.

"I know a spot where no one will see us." Now he was the bold one.

"Okay, why not?" We were two stinky boys, and I'd hear it from Mama and Boo Nanny if I dripped tunnel sludge onto our clean floors.

Past the wharf, we followed a path along the river until we came to the place where the river forked. Eagle Island was visible across the way. On our side, the wax myrtle and bay bushes had been cut away to form a clearing.

A tugboat chugged by with a cargo of logs, followed by a trail of noisy seagulls. An osprey had built a nest on one of the buoy markers. The tide was low, exposing barnacles on the pilings.

Tommy took off his clothes and leaped from the bank in a perfect swan dive. I tried to hide the fact that I didn't know how to dive and executed what Lewis called the Confederate, folding myself into a cannon-ball and hitting the water with a slap. Tommy dog-paddled to a spot where the river had washed away the bank under a tree. Half of the roots were exposed, form-ing a shelter. Tommy had a knack for finding tunnel-like spaces.

We horsed around for a while, splashing and trying to dunk each other. I was a strong swimmer—Boo Nanny had insisted on that—and I swam out toward the center of the river to impress Tommy. When I was far out, Tommy yelled, "Cops! Head for the roots!"

Tommy was closer to the bank and hid himself under the tree roots, but I was completely exposed as two Ne-gro policemen approached the clearing.

"Get out of the water," the fat one said.

While I scrambled up the bank, the second police-man walked along the river's edge and stopped at the tree with the overhanging roots. He was practically standing on Tommy's head.

I prayed that Tommy would keep quiet. He did. The only sound was the lapping of water at the bank.

The fat policeman asked me my name and age. I stood there, buck naked and dripping, with my shirt balled up in front of my privates.

"Ain't you Jack Thomas's boy?"

I looked down and nodded.

"Look at you, naked as a yard dog. You should know there's an ordinance against such."

I looked down and didn't answer. The sand was so hot, I shifted my weight from one foot to the other.

"Now put on yo' shoes so you won't be hopping around like a hen on a hot brick," he said.

I wriggled into my short pants and put on my shoes without doing up the laces.

The other policeman returned and said that he hadn't found anyone else. I felt relieved. Tommy was safe.

"This here's Jack Thomas's boy."

The other man looked at me and said, "I don't see what a boy of yo' stability would want with breaking the law."

The fat policeman said, "Now, it pains me to do this, but I'm gone have to write you up. Ah 'spects yo' daddy gone have some choice words 'bout this."

"Yessir." I hung my head in shame. It made things so much worse that these men knew my father.

He wrote out the ticket and handed it to me. "Who is with you?"

"Huh?" I said, as if hard of hearing.

"If you's smart like yo' daddy lets on you is, you gone tell me the truth, 'cause I got the distinct intuition you ain't come here wearing two pair shoes."

I looked over and saw Tommy's muddy shoes and pants in a pile. I took in a loud gulp of air. The shoes were tied with bright orange shoestrings.

"Those are my shoestrings," I said, thinking of the tree by the swimming hole where I'd left the secret gifts.

"Appears to me you ain't got a thimbleful of sense, lying the way you is."

"That's not a lie, sir." I knew I should look him directly in the eye, but I couldn't.

"Who they belong to?"

I stalled, afraid to move my eyes from their spot on the sand.

"Now I'm asking you tereckly, son. Who do those shoes belong to?" the fat policeman said. "They reek worse'n week-old mullet."

Still, I didn't answer.

"If you don't tell me, I'm gone have to give you two citations."

That was ten dollars. It was an impossibly huge sum. I didn't know how I was going to work it off. But I couldn't rat out my new friend.

"Yessir, I understand."

He handed me the second citation and motioned to follow him on the path. Before I had gotten far, the second policeman said, "Ain't you gone take the extra clothes you brought?"

He nodded toward Tommy's pile. I gathered up his clothing, but when no one was looking, I dropped his shoes and pants in the trail so Tommy wouldn't have to walk through town jaybird-naked.

At home, I waited around for Daddy to get back from work. When he found out, he was going to tan me good. He didn't do it often, but when he did, it was memorable. I hardly ever got crossways with him, and I hated disappointing him. The last time was when Lewis and I stole one of Mr. Henderson's prize watermelons and replaced it with one from Lewis's garden. Mr. Henderson's melons were known for being juicy and sweet, with few seeds. I should have known we'd get nabbed, since Mr. Henderson's melons were round and the one we left behind was oblong. Daddy did not buy the argument that it was all right because we left him a bigger one, since Mr. Henderson had not agreed to the switch.

I left the citations on the kitchen table so Daddy would see them when he came in. Boo Nanny asked what they were, and I told her.

"That ain't hardly worth fretting about. It be a dumb law to start out with—cheating young folk out of one of summer's great pleasures. That river be free as the air we breathe."

I knew Daddy would see it differently. I vowed to take my punishment like a man. My worst fear was that I might betray Tommy. It had been easy to keep Tommy a secret from the policemen. But Daddy wielded a huge power over me, and if he asked me, I was afraid I would break down and tell him, and I didn't want to do that. I wanted to protect my friend.

By the time Daddy got back from work, he already knew what I'd done. He had sources in the police department. Without looking at the citations, he called me into the parlor.

I stood in front of him. He was such a towering figure to me that I sometimes forgot how slight he actually was. But someone of small stature could do a lot of damage with the aid of a sweet-gum switch.

"What do you have to say for yourself?"

I hung my head and could see my reflection in his shoes. "Nothing."

"You broke the law." He didn't raise his voice, but

his tone indicated that it took all his discipline to keep from exploding.

"It's a stupid law," I said.

"You may not agree with the laws, but we can't govern a city if people pick and choose which laws they want to follow." As a leader of the community, he was always thinking about the greater good.

"But the river is as free as the air we breathe," I said, repeating what Boo Nanny had said.

"What if there were no laws on the river? Laws help keep order for public safety. There would be chaos—boats crashing into each other, people getting hurt."

I hung my head. We were silent for a while, and I thought I was home free. Then came the moment I had been dreading.

"And the other boy who was swimming with you. You didn't tell the police who he was."

"No, I didn't."

"Why not?"

"Because he's my friend."

Daddy took off his glasses and rubbed the corners of his eyes, as if trying to rid them of the crusty bits that collect in sleep. "I need a few moments to think about this," he said. "Wait for me in your room."

I lay down on my bed and tried to read, but I couldn't.

When he finally came to my room, he sat on the edge of the bed. I couldn't look at him, afraid I would break down, for despite my bluster, shame clung to me like the tunnel stink on my clothes.

"What you did was wrong."

"Yessir."

"You knew it was wrong, and I can't let that pass."

I leaned against the iron bedpost and waited for the next part.

"But I can't see my way to punishing you for protecting your friend. So I'll cover the second fine. But you will have to get a job and pay off your part of the fine. I'm going to switch you for your part, and your part only. So meet me at the shed in five minutes."

At that moment, I burst into tears, catching myself completely by surprise—and Daddy, too, by the looks of it. What did me in was the fairness. I had steeled myself against anger, even disappointment, but I hadn't expected fairness, and suddenly the shame and tension and fear that had been building up in me broke forth, and I found myself in front of Daddy, eyes screwed up and chest heaving. In a pathetic attempt to keep the tears inside, they came out through my nose. I was so ashamed and didn't know what to do. Daddy didn't, either, and quickly left the room.

After the switching—he had aimed at my bare legs and not my hind end—my calves stung, but I felt strangely spirited. With Daddy, it was the opposite. He went directly to bed after supper, as if the punishment had been his rather than mine.

Daddy didn't mention the incident again. A neighbor helped me get a job picking okra. The first day, I got to the field early, anxious to make a good impression. While I waited for the others to arrive, I sat under a tree and read a book. Soon a wagon of Negroes pulled up.

"Lookee there. Scholar Boy's got his nose in a book," said a man called Old Walt. I quickly stashed the book away before the others could see.

A white farmer in overalls and a straw hat announced that a fifty-cent prize would be given each week to the person who picked the most okra. He paired me with an eighteen-year-old named Ernie, a dark, handsome boy with the muscles of a man.

In the row to my other side—I couldn't believe my luck—was Julie, the prettiest of all the girls. She had bright eyes and wore her hair caught up in a yellow cloth. Some strands escaped and corked down her long neck. I felt clammy stealing a glance at her.

"You be de new boy," she said, and I felt my insides

burn, as if the sun were shining from the inside out. "You gots youself the best teacher around." She smiled at Ernie.

The okra pods grew straight up, with the tips toward the sun. Ernie showed me how to cut above the cap with a knife, leaving a little bit of the stalk. "Now, don't go messin' with the flowers. They be prime for pickin' in a few days," he said.

I followed his instructions, but the work was harder than it looked. I wanted to awe Julie with the amount of okra I could pick. My slow, clumsy hands embarrassed me.

As the pickers set to work, there was bickering and boasting along the rows. "My fingers ain't near like as supple as they used to be. But I can pick more than Scholar Boy over there," said Old Walt, who was as old as Boo Nanny.

"Who that be?" Julie said.

"De one that talks like he's voluntary white folks," he said.

I buried my head among the leaves. Crouched down, I glanced at Julie through the stalks. She bent over to reach some low-growing pods, and her dress gaped at the neck. Keeping my eyes on her, I slit my thumb with the knife. "Ouch!" I cried, and whipped my hand back and forth. It stung something awful.

Julie stopped. "You okay, Scholar Boy?"

When she called me that, it sounded like music. I wanted to be Scholar Boy for the rest of my life.

She came over to see if there was any blood. "This'll fix you right up." I felt her soft, warm mouth on my thumb. My entire insides felt weightless. She returned to her row. I was in high spirits. I could do this for the entire season, no problem.

A woman at the far end of the field started singing, and soon other voices joined in. We worked all morning under the high blue sky.

By midday, Julie was far up the row, and Ernie had already moved on to another part of the field. The high spirits of the morning had faded. Now I was stuck working next to a fat girl who had been hit with the ugly stick. My back ached, and my fingers were red and itching from the whiskers on the outside of the okra pods. I hadn't brought gloves or a hat like the rest of the workers.

When the others broke for lunch, I kept on going. "That boy ain't lazy," I heard someone say.

Truth was, I wanted to catch up to Julie. It made me happy to work beside her. The next day, I planned to bring her a bouquet of flowers from our garden.

After lunch, Ernie came over and said, "You ain't had a thing in yo' stomach all day."

"I'm behind," I said.

"I'll fix that," he said, and took over for me.

His hands flew over the plant, cutting the pods with incredible speed and putting them in my basket, not his.

After I wolfed down a couple of pieces of corn bread and returned, Ernie gave me back my row. But even with his help, I fell behind and didn't see much of Julie until the end of the day, when I stood in line behind her and Ernie while the farmer's son weighed each basket.

It was sunset, and the clouds had turned golden. "They's fine as Sis' Julie's skin there," said a worker Ernie's age.

"Go way, niggar. You better not be casting sheep eyes at my gal's skin," Ernie said.

I felt my stomach seize up. Of course. Julie was Ernie's sweetheart. What a fool I had been. I should have guessed it.

I emptied my basket into the wagon, disappointed to see that I had picked less okra than Old Walt. I'd have given anything for Julie to be somewhere else instead of looking on.

Ernie patted me on the shoulder. "Don't you worry. This be yo' first day."

He and Julie left together, giggling and horsing around. I trudged home, stiff as an old man.

The following days were pure drudgery. By week's end, it was clear that Ernie was the top picker. No one else came close. On payday, I made sure to be near the front of the line. When the farmer's son paid me, I pocketed the coins and smoothed out the crinkles in the bills. I couldn't wait to deliver the cash into Daddy's hand, to pay off part of my debt. As I strutted down the line, Ernie pulled me aside. "I 'spect the boss man be shavin' me," he said in a low voice, not wanting the others to hear. He glanced around him, then said even lower, "If you could see your way fit to check his figures, I'd be mighty obliged."

"Well, you worked six days, so at sixty cents a day, you should get three-sixty, plus a fifty-cent bonus for best picker. So he owes you four-ten," I told him. I wished Julie was there to hear me, but she had already collected her pay and was waiting for Ernie under the tree.

He returned to his place. I hung around the wagon and waited for him to get to the front of the line. He shifted his bare feet in the sand as the farmer's son counted out the money.

"Here's three-twenty, including the bonus," said the scrawny white boy.

"But I worked from de rising to de setting of the sun." Ernie held his hat in his hand and hung his head low.

"And we 'preciate your work, we do."

"So dat be three-sixty, plus the prize money." He got flustered, forgetting the numbers. I whispered the amount to him and moved away. "Four-ten, all told," he said.

The farmer's son glowered at me. Ernie held his head down so far that the knob at the top of his spine stood out, glossy brown, like a pine knot on a well-worn floor. "I just want my due," he said, keeping his eyes on his feet.

"You take what we give you, or find work elsewhere," the son said.

At that moment the farmer came up behind his son. "Are you out of your mind?" the older man said. "That buck picks twice the amount of a regular field hand. You give him his fair wages."

The son frowned and handed Ernie another dollar. "There's a little extree," he said.

Ernie took the money and made a deep bow. Hat in hand, he walked backward and made several smaller bows, thanking the farmer again and again as he bobbed like a county fair water decoy, waiting to be shot.

I tried to blend in with the other pickers by the wagon, but the farmer's son pointed at me. "There's your trouble-maker. That smarty right there."

"Get over here, boy," the farmer said.

I was shaking as I approached. I reached in my pocket and felt my money. He couldn't take it back. I wouldn't let him.

"We won't be needing your help anymore," the older man said. The son gave a smug smile.

"I'm sorry. I didn't mean to cause trouble. I won't do it again," I said, desperation in my voice.

"It's a little late for that," the son said. "Now get out of here. You're a lousy picker anyway."

I left without saying good-bye to Ernie or Julie. Old Walt followed me to the gate. "Scholar Boy, you ain't got the sense God gave a stump," he said. "You gots to learn to humble down and lay shut-mouth."

The money in my pocket that had made me feel so rich now made me feel poor, because it was half of what I needed and now I had no job. I was such a good-for-nothing worker that I had been fired. On the way home, I dawdled to delay the moment I had to tell Daddy.

But when I did, he was completely understanding. He said that I had learned my lesson, and he would forgive the rest of my debt.

When I told Boo Nanny, she hummed under her breath as she listened, the way she did in church in response to the preacher's sermon. "Bad times a-comin'," she said.

"Things aren't so bad," I said. Now that Daddy had let me off the hook, I didn't count getting fired as something bad, not on the scale she meant.

"Don't crow till you get out de woods. There might be a bear behind the last tree," she said.

FIVE

"I got a hankering to see the ocean. I reckon I's earned myself some time off," Boo Nanny announced, and I knew that the day I looked forward to every summer had arrived. She worked seven days a week, but every year she took one day off and we went to the beach together.

She put on a floppy straw hat and got her walking stick. I carried a tin pail full of corn bread, beans, ham hocks, collard greens, and two pieces of blueberry pie.

It took the entire morning to reach the shore. Once we passed through the dunes, Boo Nanny unlaced her cracked leather high tops, knotted her long skirt at the knees, and walked toward the ocean. Her toes were as bent as her back and left misshapen claw prints in the sand, like a creature from one of her ghost stories.

We ate lunch, then she combed the beach for shells.

Even though her bent back put her head closer to the ground, she still leaned even farther to look for shells.

I never found anything. I didn't have the patience to look. While she sifted through a drift of crushed shells at the high-tide mark, I plopped down on the wet sand where the waves washed up. Minnows flickered, silver at the edge of the sea. A group of willets played in the yellow foam, hopping about as if in a bubble bath.

As the water pulled back, I dug and came up with a handful of wet sand that contained dozens of tiny butterfly shells, closed like praying hands. The creatures inside burrowed against my palms, tickling. I let the water run through my cupped hands and wash away the sand, leaving only the beautifully colored shells—orange and pink like the beginning of a sunset, purple and gray like the end. I put them in the tin pail. Back home, when we boiled the shells for soup, they would open up in the shape of butterflies.

My family ate almost everything from the sea—crabs, oysters, mussels, clams, fish, and shrimp. But we were never, ever to eat a turtle egg. On that point, Boo Nanny was perfectly clear. The giant sea turtles laid their eggs on the shore in the full moon of June, and the eggs, considered a delicacy, sometimes found their way to the market. "How's that mama gone keep her family alive if the likes of you is snacking on her babies?" she said.

Boo Nanny returned with a full pie tin of olive shells, angel wings, baby's ears, kitten's paws, and jingle shells in shades of silver, gold, and black. "Looky here," she said, and held up a hank of seaweed that had, tangled in its fronds, a black leathery pouch with horns at the four corners. "This here's a devil's purse. For baby skates. It keeps the little ones safe till they hatch."

I had seen the odd-looking fish washed up on shore. It was shaped like a kite and had a stiff spike for a tail. Was it possible that this huge fish started out life in that tiny pouch? Boo Nanny showed me the slit along the side of the case where the baby fish escaped when they were ready.

She grew up on a plantation by the ocean and knew an awful lot for someone who couldn't read or write. She taught me things that Daddy, with all his degrees, didn't know: that the full moon pulls the tides higher; that star formations appear in different parts of the sky depending on the season; that conch shells hold the sound of the ocean inside them; that the tiny beads of silver that twinkle at the water's edge are actually alive.

"How do you know these things?" I asked, carefully unhooking the devil's pouch from the seaweed. I would dry it out and add it to the treasures on my windowsill.

"I use my own two eyes. All you gots to do is look.

Now, your daddy could talk a possum out of a tree, but sometimes he can't see what's dead straight in front of his nose if it ain't in a book. Knowing's first and foremost 'bout seeing what's in front of you," she said.

The walk to the shore was always easier than the walk back. Each year the journey got a little harder for Boo Nanny, and this year was the hardest of all. We had to stop many times to rest. Even with all her potions and tonics, she was getting weaker and more bent over. I wasn't sure how many more years she would be able to make the trip.

"I likes it when you read to me. Makes the work go nice and easy-like," Boo Nanny said, speaking through teeth clamped over several wooden clothespins.

I could hardly see the print for the sweat in my eyes. After I finished the story, I closed the book and used it like a pillow as I stretched out in the shade of the hanging clothes, hoping the edges of the wet sheet would graze my face. There was not a whiff of breeze, and the air was sticky and buggy.

"When can we start our lessons? After school starts, I won't have much time," I said, gazing up at the white panels above me. All summer, I'd been trying to convince her to let me teach her to read, but she was better at finding excuses than I was at avoiding Sunday school.

"Cocoa Baby, I loves you to pieces, but you's gone be the death of me with you crazy ideas," she said after removing the remaining clothespins from her mouth.

"Why don't you want to learn to read?" I asked.

Daddy believed that the only way to improve our race was through education. But if I mentioned Daddy to Boo Nanny, she would take the opposite side, for no other reason than to be ornery.

"I's too set in my ways and don't see no call for it, at my age."

"Suppose you wanted to go to the drugstore instead of the shoe shop."

"I be old and bent, but I ain't stupid. All I gots to do is look in the window. If I sees a line of leather high tops, I'm right nigh certain I ain't gone be buying no borax there."

"But if the shades are down."

"Then I just looks at that big old shoe cut out of wood over the front door and knows this ain't the place."

She was trying my patience.

"Wouldn't you like to be able to read the street signs?"

"I knows every street in this town that I be wanting to walk on."

"What about the Bible? Wouldn't it be nice to read it on your own?"

She folded a sun-starched pillowcase and held it to

her chest. The glare off the white sheets made her damp face shine.

"I ain't rightly considered that," she said, and for a moment I thought I had won her over. But then she waved a pillowcase at me and said, "Now shoo. I be pure-t tired of your nattering."

That evening, I talked to Daddy out of her hearing. "For every reason I come up with, she has an excuse. What is it she's afraid of?"

"Failing," he said.

"What?"

"It's hard for you to understand, son, but try to put yourself in her shoes. She grew up as a slave, when it was against the law to teach Negroes to read and write. She spent her formative years in bondage. Your grandmother is an amazing woman, but when you're bought and sold like a mule, treated like dirt, told you're inferior, and taken advantage of in ways you can't begin to imagine, it's hard to develop any self-confidence."

I was dumbfounded. Did Boo Nanny have any idea how much Daddy respected her? Maybe her conflicts with him were all in her mind.

"What should I do, then?" I asked.

"Ask her for fifteen minutes a day. Anyone can find fifteen minutes."

"She'll think of some reason she doesn't have the time."

"Okay, then tell her I'll do the supper dishes for her."

"You'd do that?"

"Of course."

I ran to tell Boo Nanny about Daddy's offer, and for the first time in the eleven years I'd known her, she was without words. Finally she smiled broadly and said, "That man be willing to put his hands in de suds for this here cranky in-law?"

"That's what he said."

"That'd be a sight for sore eyes."

"I take it that's a yes."

She nodded, then said, "He better not go ruining those cuffs I starched so nice and stiff for him."

We started in the living room that evening when there was still plenty of light.

I got out a pencil and tablet and wrote the first letter of the alphabet, printing it on two lines. "This is an *A*. And this is a *B*," I said, and repeated myself several times.

I pointed to the first letter and said, "What's that?"

She squinted and pulled the paper so close her nose was almost touching. Then she held it at arm's length and squinted.

I made the letters bigger. "Can you see that?" She

shook her head. I tried again, this time using six lines. "What about that?"

"Chile, my tired ol' eyes can't get down that small."

Suddenly I realized: she was practically blind. For all I knew, she had been that way for years, and no one noticed because she left the sewing and darning to Mama.

"No problem," I said cheerfully. "I know just what we'll do." I refused to give her any cause to quit. No way was I going to let her fail.

"This won't take long. I'll let you know when I'm done," I said.

She picked up a dust rag while I grabbed some newspapers from the back porch. We saved them to use as kindling and for private business in the privy. Ever since the *Record* went from a weekly to a daily, we couldn't use the papers fast enough, and they piled up on the back porch.

I cut out both capital and little letters for the first five letters of the alphabet, then laid them on the rug. The capital letters were about a foot high. When I was done, she sat back in the chair. Because she was bent over, she was at the perfect angle to see the letters. I went over the names and sounds with her several times.

"Now de big C and de little *c*, that makes perfect sense. One be de spittin' image of t'other, like a mama and her baby chile. But that mama *A* ain't nothing similar to the baby *a*. Same goes for the *e*."

I knew if I showed any impatience she would refuse to go on. "Do you ever ask yourself why the color red is red?" I asked. "There's no reason. That's just the way it is. Same with the alphabet. If you think too hard, you'll get yourself all tangled up. So just try to memorize it."

I decided to simplify and work only with capital letters.

After she learned the first five, I cut out a duplicate *D* and moved the floppy newsprint letters around to form words: *BAD, BED, DAB, DEAD.*

I went over the words, and she repeated them. When I rearranged the letters to spell *DEAD*, she stared at them for a long time, then said, "That don't make a lick of sense. It oughta be *DED*, just like *BED*." She removed the *A* from the letters I had assembled on the rug.

"Well, it's not."

"Well, it oughta be."

I returned the *A* to its original place. I wished I hadn't chosen that example, but I was having trouble coming up with words that used only the first five letters of the alphabet. "The correct spelling is D-E-A-D. Dead."

"You is sure?"

"You have to trust me," I said, but then started to doubt myself. The more I stared at the letters on the floor, the stranger they became, like no word I'd ever seen. My mind was playing tricks on me.

I opened up the dictionary to check the word. There, in the *D*s, I found a dollar bill stuck in the crease. I held it up for Boo Nanny.

"Here's the last of Mama's organ money. We hid it in the dictionary," I said.

"You mean to tell me if I done took it into my head to educate myself afore this, I might find myself in possession of a raft of cash money?" she said.

"Here it is . . . d-e-a-d. Correctly spelled," I said, and held my finger under the word in the dictionary, but her eyes couldn't focus on anything that small.

"When they lays this old sack o' bones belowground, I want my gravestone to read: Josephine August. D-E-A-D. And that's what I's gone be, Cocoa Baby, if we don't stop this lesson right now."

I was surprised to see that almost an hour had passed.

The following day, I was tickled when Boo Nanny wanted to have two sessions. After lunch, I started cutting out the next five letters of the alphabet. As I cut into the newspaper to make an *H*, an article caught my eye. It was an editorial by Alex Manly, the owner of Daddy's paper, in the August 18 edition. I put down the scissors and started to read.

The editorial was titled "Mrs. Felton's Speech." I had

never heard of Mrs. Felton—I guessed she was the wife of a representative from Georgia, judging from the editorial. What caught my eye was the part of her speech that caused Mr. Manly to respond in an editorial. I read it several times, trying to understand: "If it takes lynching to protect woman's dearest possession from the ravening human beasts, then I say lynch a thousand times a week if necessary."

I was stumped by the phrase "dearest possession." As for lynching, I had heard the word and knew it was something bad, but didn't know exactly what.

I opened the dictionary and marked the place with the dollar bill. The definition—to execute without due process of law—put me no closer to understanding. I depended on words to be a window on understanding, but it was proving to be a mighty cloudy window.

"Ain't you got no upbringing?" Boo Nanny said when I closed the dictionary and returned to the article. "Read that article out loud."

Stumbling over some of the words, I read: "Every Negro lynched is called a big, burly black brute, when in fact many of those who have thus been dealt with had white men for their fathers and were not only not black and burly but were sufficiently attractive for white girls of culture and refinement to fall in love with them."

Rocking in her chair, Boo Nanny murmured, "That ain't gone sit well."

I was perplexed by the meaning but continued, as the editor addressed Mrs. Felton: "Tell your men that it is no worse for a black man to be intimate with a white woman than for a white man to be intimate with a colored woman."

"Sweet Jesus." Boo Nanny frowned and shook her head. "Big trouble's a-brewing."

"Why?" I said, heading back to the dictionary.

"We take they jobs, it's bad enough, but all hell's gone jolt loose if we start marrying 'em."

I looked up *intimate* in the dictionary. There were two entries—one a verb, the other an adjective, and each pronounced a different way. One meant "to communicate indirectly," and the other meant "belonging to one's deepest nature." I puzzled over the two meanings. What did either have to do with marriage? I couldn't square the definition with what I was reading.

I felt ashamed. I was supposed to be the championship reader, yet I couldn't make heads or tails of the editorial even after looking up the vocabulary I didn't know. And Boo Nanny seemed to grasp it immediately, though she didn't know half the words.

Mr. Manly's editorial ended with an address to white men: "You set yourselves down as a lot of carping hypocrites in that you cry aloud for the virtue of your women while you seek to destroy the morality of ours."

"What's that big book there say for *hypocrite?*" Boo Nanny said.

"I know that one. It's like the churchgoer who talks about honesty and turns around and robs you blind."

"Yep. The pews be filled with folks aplenty like that." She smiled. "And the lot of 'em won't have the foggiest what I be talking 'bout if I calls 'em that."

That evening over dessert, I brought up the editorial and asked Daddy to explain it. He asked me how I knew about it, and I told him.

"This be the first I heared of it," Mama said.

"You remember Alex Manly, the paper's editor? The man who showed you the printing press?" he asked me.

I nodded.

"Well, a society woman made a speech that was reprinted nationwide, and Mr. Manly took issue with what she said. He responded with an editorial that hit a raw nerve in the white community."

"What is lynching, Daddy?" I said.

"Jack," Mama said with a note of warning in her voice.

"It's part of his education, Sadie," Daddy said, wiping his mouth and placing the napkin by his plate.

"Leave that boy be a boy. There's time aplenty for him to learn unpleasant things," Mama said, but Daddy didn't listen.

"Sometimes men get·together in groups, and a herd mentality develops and they do things they wouldn't do individually," he said. He spoke slowly, considering every word. "You've probably seen that on the playground, with children ganging up and bullying a schoolmate. Alone, it's harder for an individual to be hateful, eye to eye, to his fellow man."

He had said something similar when I apologized to that Dry Ponder for stealing his son's bike. That man was plenty hateful, and it didn't make a lick of difference that I was eye to eye with him.

"When men attribute qualities to others that take away a person's dignity—words like *brute* or *beast*—it's easier to treat that person as less than human. A mob can develop a mind of its own and act in ways that fly in the face of justice," Daddy said.

"Like what?" I asked.

"That child don't need to know about such hateful things," Mama said.

"I'm trying to explain lynching in a way that makes sense," Daddy said.

"You find that way, you be sure to let me in on de education," Boo Nanny said.

"So why did this white society woman suggest lynching?" I asked, still unclear exactly what lynching was.

Daddy took a deep breath. "Well, Mrs. Felton thought that white men needed to do a better job of protecting their women in the countryside from the, um, unwanted attentions of black men."

"That doesn't sound so bad," I said.

"She was talking about violent attentions."

"You mean rape?" I asked.

Mama gasped.

"Do you know what that word means?" Daddy asked.

I shook my head no.

"Well, it involves unwanted sex. . . ."

"Hush up. That ain't no thing for young ears," Mama said.

"He deserves to have his questions answered," Daddy said.

"Jackson . . ." When Mama gave Daddy that dark look and drew out the syllables in his name, I knew she would not be refused. She turned to me and said, "Run along now, Moses. You be excused."

There was no reason to treat me like a child. I knew about sex; Lewis had told me. Men and women got together and had sex and made babies. Lewis's next-door neighbor, a white woman named Mrs. Roberts, was a sex maniac, because she had six children and had done it six times.

I made a big deal of shutting the door to my room but remained in the hall. After a few moments, I flattened myself against the wall by the kitchen door and listened, but they had moved on to other topics.

"All of the white advertisers pulled out to protest the editorial," Daddy was saying.

"What you doing depending on white folk for?" Boo Nanny said. "Feed you with de corn, choke you with de cob."

"It's a good deal for them. Our paper helps them reach a whole new market. We're the only Negro daily in the South."

"You stay in awe of de white man, he got you round his thumb, just what like in slavery," she said.

"We need to find people in our community to pick up the slack. Josephine, would you be willing to ask your minister if he could take out an ad temporarily, until the ruckus dies down?"

"You ain't seed fit to darken the door, but you come with you hat in hand when you's in a pickle," she grumbled.

That was a regular cause of bickering between Boo Nanny and Daddy—she went to Sunday school and church every week, and he refused to go.

"If we don't find more ads, the paper's going to have to shut down. You wouldn't believe the uproar this has caused. Letters have poured in, demanding that Alex be horsewhipped and run out of town."

"Jack, you fixin' to lose your job? Things is tight enough as they is." I could hear fear in Mama's voice.

"No, no, nothing of the sort. That's why I didn't mention it. I didn't want you to worry. This will blow over."

"You mention purity of white womanhood and de black man in de same breath, and you got big trouble. That editor be swinging afore it's over," Boo Nanny said.

"Shhh," Mama said.

"He's gone," Daddy said.

There was a moment of silence at the table, then Mama said, "Moses? You there?"

I stood perfectly still and didn't say a word, praying she wouldn't get up. She didn't.

"That Mrs. Felton don't get herself exercised none over the brutality our womens endure at the hand of the white man. This mixing done humiliated us, tore our families apart, and some society lady has the nerve to suggest that their precious womanhood be at risk. That woman be a hypocrite!" Boo Nanny said.

"Where did you learn that word?" Daddy asked, impressed.

"My grandboy. And come next year, I be spelling it as well."

The hubbub over the editorial forced the *Record* to move its office from above the saloon by the wharf. That Saturday, I helped Daddy move the newspaper to its new home on Seventh Street, above the Love and Charity Benevolent Society, a Negro organization that raised money for hospitals and sick people.

We arrived early at the Water Street office and woke up the crumpled white sailor who had spent the night underneath the outdoor stairs that led to the *Record*.

Reporters, compositors, and pressmen all turned out to help so the paper would not have to suspend publication for more than one day. Everyone wore work clothes except for Mr. Manly, who wore a coat, tie, starched shirt, and hat.

It took several wagonloads to move the typewriters, desks, and office supplies. The last thing to go was the monster press. Now silent, it required six men to hoist it onto the stairs, slide it along the railings, and lift it onto the wagon. I thought of the press as a big, burly black brute.

Around eleven, I took a break and sat on the edge of the porch of the saloon. A stocky man with a sandy-colored handlebar mustache was sweeping before the saloon opened at noon. He wore a white shirt with garters above the elbow to keep his cuffs from getting dirty. He smiled at me, and I moved to the corner so he could sweep under the spot where I'd been sitting.

A white businessman approached him and asked where he could find Mr. Manly.

The saloon keeper pointed out the man in a suit and hat by the wagon.

"No, I'm looking for a colored man," the businessman said.

"That is Mr. Manly. He just looks white," he said, and then called the editor over to the porch.

The man—evidently the building owner—had come to collect September's rent.

"We won't be here in September," Mr. Manly said.

"The lease runs through the end of the year, and I expect for you to do the honorable thing," the owner said.

"I would have gladly stayed in place and paid rent for the rest of the year, but because of the outcry over the editorial, you requested that I leave immediately, and I have honored that request. You can't ask me to break the lease and then hold me to it at the same time."

"Well, I never . . . ," the owner sputtered.

"Now, if you'll excuse me, I have a paper to move. Good day."

"Did you hear that? Did you hear the way that colored spoke to me?" the owner said after Mr. Manly left.

"I'm not sure I know what you mean. Mr. Manly has never been anything if not polite," the saloon keeper said.

"Give them a little power and that's what you get. Insolence like that deserves a good thrashing."

"I'm sorry, sir, but I'm not following. You asked him to vacate the building, and he complied with your request. What is your complaint?"

"That uppity attitude."

"I've collected rent for you for the past year, and Mr. Manly has never once been late. He's as trustworthy as any man I know."

"As trustworthy as any colored man you know," the owner corrected him.

"That's not what I said," the saloon keeper insisted. He picked up his broom and continued sweeping, and I slunk away, unnoticed.

SIX

More than anything in the world, I wanted a bike. With my own wheels, I could go to the ocean anytime I wanted. I could also visit Daddy at the newspaper, come home at second recess, or ride to the forest and collect plants for Boo Nanny's potions. With a bike, I might be Lewis's best friend again. He went riding with Johnny, and since I didn't have wheels, I was left out. Christmas was only four months away, but I knew there wasn't a chance I'd get wheels.

When I was younger, I thought Santy Claw was a cheapskate man in a red suit who didn't care for the likes of me but favored rich folks like Lewis, who got a bike when he asked for one. When I found out that old Santy Claw was none other than my daddy, I was relieved, because I knew with certainty that no matter what I asked for, I would get socks and a flannel shirt and maybe an orange.

The last week of August, I went to the hardware store to check out their wheels. The hardware store sold screws and nails, paint, fishing tackle, ropes, fishing nets, sails, and anchors. But I was only interested in the bikes.

I went inside the store without stopping at the counter to gaze at the big glass jars of red licorice sticks, peppermint candies, and lemon drops. In the back corner stood four shiny new Eagle bicycles on sale. The most expensive model was $30. It had a lantern, a leather seat, and baskets on the back. The cheapest model was $18. Even at the sale price, I could never afford it.

As I ran my hand over the cold shiny handlebars, the burly owner approached. He had curly muttonchops in the shape of New Jersey. (Lewis had a map in his room, and I had memorized all forty-five states.)

Mr. New Jersey wore red sleeve garters above the elbow. His chin rolled over his stiff collar like the top of a muffin. He wore wireless glasses like Daddy, but his did not make him look smart.

"Stand back. Don't touch the merchandise," the man said in a gruff voice, and I stepped away, backing into a barrel of nails and causing a few to jump over the sides. I swept them into my hand and returned them to the barrel. Mr. New Jersey watched me closely to make sure I didn't pocket any. He took the cake for pure low-down meanness.

At that moment, a father and son approached the bikes. I stood in the corner by the crab traps and watched the little blond boy. He wore the kind of sailor outfit that was the style among the better classes. With all that fair skin and light hair, he could have been a ghost. He was maybe a couple of years younger than me—I'm not good at guessing the age of white boys. But I recognized the spark in his eyes as he gazed in awe and wonder at the bikes.

"May I help you?" the owner asked. He could be polite when he wanted to.

"We're just looking, thanks," the father said.

Mr. New Jersey frowned in my direction and said, "Is he bothering you? I can ask him to leave."

"No, he's fine," the father said.

I listened as the owner described the features of the newest models, which were even more beautiful than the bikes Lewis and Johnny owned.

The little sailor mounted the most expensive bike. It was too big for him, and his feet barely touched the ground.

"Would you like to take the bike for a spin?" the owner asked.

"No, we're just seeing what's available for now," the father said, and winked. I knew in my heart that the boy would wake up on Christmas Day and find a bike under the tree. He was still too young to know the true identity of Santy Claw.

The boy ran his chubby hands along the handlebars, leaving fingerprints all over the shiny metal.

When they left the store, I knew I had to move on before the owner yelled at me. On the way out, I saw, taped on the glass of the door, a poster advertising a contest. A free bicycle would be given to the person under eighteen who came up with the best advertisement for an Eagle bicycle.

I felt my heart quicken. I had a chance to win a bike! I wouldn't have to be left out when Lewis and Johnny rode their bikes. The deadline was in three weeks.

The contest would be judged on the idea and the slogan, not drawing ability, which was a good thing, since I couldn't draw worth a lick. But I loved words. I liked to play with them, learn new ones, and put them together in different ways. I felt confident that I could come up with a good advertisement.

School started in September, but the first month, I didn't have much homework and had plenty of time to work on the project. Over the next few weeks, I tried and discarded many ideas. The best ones I tried out on both Boo Nanny and Daddy. Their opinions were always so far apart that I figured if I came up with something that pleased both of them, I'd have a winner for sure. I read my favorite slogan aloud to Boo Nanny: "Eagle bikes. The best mechanics, the best material, the best model, the best adjustment."

"Too many words," she said. "Folks ain't gone trust you if you carry on till you ain't got a breath left. A man tells me how honest he is, I keep an eagle eye on my valuables."

"Eagle eye," I mused. "I wonder if there's something there."

She shook her head. "Too common."

Though we were making progress in our lessons, Boo Nanny could barely read. I figured that was why she preferred a slogan with fewer words. But Daddy said, "She's right. The shorter the better. Every word has to count."

They never agreed on anything, but they were both in perfect harmony that my slogan was not up to snuff.

Over the next few weeks, I tried out many more ideas, and nothing seemed to catch their fancy. Finally, two days before the deadline, I came up with an idea that everyone liked. I sketched it out and took it to the hardware store that same afternoon.

I was relieved to find behind the counter a nice-looking woman with light brown hair in a bun. She had a small waist and big shoulders that made her head look small.

I tried to keep my hand from shaking as I held out my entry. It had taken me three weeks to come up with five words. That was a word and two-thirds per week. At that rate—eighty-seven words per year—it would take me four years to finish a single newspaper article. Daddy wrote them in one day. Writing was definitely not the profession for me.

"This is for the contest," I said in a weak voice.

"Pardon?" the woman said, ignoring the folded piece of paper I clutched in my hand.

I repeated myself, a little louder.

She moved her eyebrows together, still not understanding.

"For the bicycle," I said.

"Oh," she said in sudden recognition. Then she paused and looked concerned. "Well, I'm . . . Let me check on the rules. I'm not sure what kinds of people are eligible."

"You have to be under eighteen," I said, pointing to the poster taped on the front door. I was six years away from the cutoff. Surely she could see that I qualified.

"Yes, I know, but . . . there may be . . . well, there could be other restrictions. Let me see what you've got."

With shaking hands, I gave her the folded paper. She opened it and stared for what seemed like minutes. What was taking her so long? It was only five words.

The picture showed a boy on a bike with wings on the back wheels. The neat block letters read: RIDE AN EAGLE AND SOAR.

She clucked her tongue and raised her eyebrows in surprise. "Mmm. Not bad." She peered down at me. "This is actually very clever. Did you think of this?"

"My Boo . . . my grandmother helped me," I said.

"Your grandmother?"

I nodded. "She only said if she liked it or not. I came up with the phrase myself."

"I see."

"So you'll accept it?" I said.

"This breaks my heart, but . . ."

I felt bad news coming, but I held her gaze. Then she softened.

"Just a minute. Let me check with my husband and see if we can make an exception."

She turned her head and raised her voice. "Fred, there's a young man here with an entry for the bicycle contest."

From the stockroom came a deep voice: "The deadline's not for another two days. Results will be posted Saturday."

"Yes, but . . . could you come out here and take a look? We have a special situation."

The man came out. As I feared, it was the man with

sideburns shaped like New Jersey. He must have remembered me, because he took one look at me and said, "I'm sorry, but we already have too many entries."

"The deadline isn't until day after tomorrow," I said boldly.

"There's nothing in the rules that says . . . ," the woman said.

"Judith, let me handle this."

He hated me because I had touched his bicycles.

"But he's a nice, clean young man."

With Sadie as a mother, I had the corner on cleanliness, for sure. Neighbors called her Shine-'em-up Sadie because her pots were so clean. But I wondered what that had to do with anything.

"Take a look. This is quite good," the woman said.

"You know as well as I do that we can't . . ."

"It's not going to hurt you to take a look," the kind woman said.

He took the piece of paper from her. I relaxed a little. Despite the bad drawing, I could tell that he liked it.

"Eagles . . . soar. Hmmm." He looked at me suspiciously. "Did you copy this from somewhere?"

My mouth had totally dried out and words lodged in my throat, as if I had swallowed a handful of butterfly shells. I wanted to explain to him that I had been with Boo Nanny that very morning and had seen a hawk soaring in the sky. The slogan came to me in a flash. After trying and discarding so many ideas, I knew in an instant that I had come up with the winning slogan. But Mr. New Jersey seemed so hostile that I couldn't get the words out. All I could do was shake my head no.

"Are you sure?"

I shook my head again.

"Fred, there's no harm in . . ."

"Okay, boy. Leave the entry here. The winner will be posted on Saturday."

I left feeling happy. I could tell that both the husband and wife had liked my entry, and that made four adults, counting Boo Nanny and Daddy. I didn't know who the judges were or how many other people had entered the contest, but I felt hopeful.

I didn't tell Lewis about the contest. My family were the only people who knew, and they warned me not to get my hopes up, but it was hard. My slogan was good. I knew it.

The next few days passed slowly. Finally Saturday arrived, and I willed myself to stay away from the hardware store until noon. Then I walked the long way, going by the docks before swinging back around to the store. The air was filled with the unpleasant smell of pogie meal from the fertilizer factory.

Luckily, no one was in front of the window where the

winners were posted. I approached slowly. Before I even got close enough to read, I felt my body react in the same place as when I saw the hawk. Only this time, it was dark behind my rib cage, where before it was light. I didn't win. I didn't even get honorable mention, though a bicycle lamp wouldn't have done me much good without a bicycle.

The winner was a seventeen-year-old boy. His slogan was "Eagle Bicycles. Tried and True. Superior Quality. Distinctive Features."

I'd never buy a bicycle from an ad like that. But then again, I'd never buy a bicycle at all. Not even on sale.

In my effort to contain the sobs, my stomach lurched as if I had the hiccups.

I wanted to leave before anyone caught me being a bad sport, which was the worse thing you could be, in Daddy's book. But before I could get away, the owner's wife saw me through the window and came outside.

"Don't be discouraged," she said. "You had very tough competition."

I wanted to reply to the kind woman, but I couldn't speak without sobbing. So I turned my back to her and ran away as fast as I could.

The following week, I awoke to sheets of rain slapping against the windowpanes so hard the frames shook. As

I was getting dressed, Boo Nanny came to my room and told me that I had to stay home.

"I can't miss school," I said. Mama and Daddy had already left for work.

"Lord a mercy, honey, you ain't gone out in this mess. It's a hurricane for true." Wind whipped the tops of the trees, and the rain fell so fast that water gushed along the road, making trenches in the sand and shooshing brown leaves and pine needles in its flow.

"How do you know? It could just be a hard rain."

"I knows a hurricane when I sees one. When the trees gets to leaning over same way like my back, I don't need to wait for your daddy to come home with stories about roofs blown off, windows broken, flooding."

"It's even more important that I go to school when it rains," I said. The roof leaked at our school, and my new teacher, Mr. Barker, depended on me to put buckets under the drips on the second floor.

"People gets theyself killed in hurricanes," she said.

"But this isn't a hurricane," I insisted.

"Something be wrong with you, Cocoa Baby, if you wants to get out in this blow."

"I can't miss school, I just can't," I pleaded. I was going for perfect attendance for the sixth year in a row.

"Ain't nobody but a fool goes out in a toad floater like this."

"A little water isn't going to hurt me."

"I been out in a hurricane. It ain't just plain ol' wind and rain. It be a monster, like the plat-eye. It gone hop on your neck and ride you like you an ol' mule."

"I'm going to school. I don't care what you say," I said.

"Don't you be talking back at me like you got no upbringing. I said you ain't going and you ain't going." She stamped her foot on the floor.

I had no choice but to stay home. It turned out not to be a hurricane, just a bad storm. I spent the day bored and sulking.

When Daddy got home from work, I complained to him. He said he'd have a few words with Boo Nanny.

After supper, while Mama was washing the dishes, Daddy caught Boo Nanny as she was headed out the door to church.

"School's important to him," Daddy explained. "I don't want anything to stand between him and learning. In the future, I don't want you to keep him home from school."

Boo Nanny looked hurt. I was sorry I had complained to Daddy. "If you think an unlettered old crow like me can't see the use in a good education, you be wrong. But this morning, it was blowing something awful."

"It's still coming down hard and you're on your way to Bible study."

"Ain't raining nothing like what it was."

"All I'm saying is church is important to you, and you don't let a little rain hold you back."

"You'd be a sight better off if you tended to your soul with the git up and git you use on your mind."

"Let's not go into that now. You know we don't agree on these things."

But it was too late. They were bickering about his refusal to go to church.

I felt bad I had set them off. It didn't take much. They were always at odds with each other, with Mama making peace. But before she could break up this argument, Daddy stalked off to his room in a huff, and Boo Nanny slammed the door on her way to Bible study.

Mama dried her hands, put away the dish towel, and asked me to come with her to the parlor.

"I wish they wouldn't quarrel. I don't think they like each other," I said.

"Don't fret so hard, honey. The honest-to-God real reason they quarrel is they's too much alike. Both stubborn as they come. Won't give an inch. Does it make you sad?"

I nodded. I felt I had to side with one, but was loyal to both.

"Don't be all tore up about this. To see you like this pure hurts me to the bone. Come here and sit beside me." I crawled next to her and leaned against her shoulder. She drew me closer. "The thing to keep in your head is they both loves you to pieces."

"But which one's right?"

"Right ain't got nothing to do with it, baby. Different. If you had yourself a box of candy, would you refuse a lemon drop 'cause it ain't the same as licorice? No, you got a sweet tooth, so you take both. Now, your daddy's the smartest man I know, but for all his book learning, he couldn't tell the difference between a buzzard and a crow. He's a modern man, always looking ahead. Boo Nanny favors the old ways, the stories and cures and superstitions from slave days, passed down from Africa by mouth 'cause folks couldn't write."

"If she thinks the stories are so important, why won't she talk about growing up as a slave?"

"Too much sadness and heartache. She doesn't want you to worry yourself with something that's past."

"Do you remember what it was like?"

"I was a little tiny baby."

"But I want to know."

"I know, honey, I know. I've tried till I'm blue in the face to get her to tell me about my daddy—your granddaddy—but all she'll say is he was sold south before I was born—in the month of August."

She explained that when the war ended, Boo Nanny

left the plantation with only the clothes on her back, a rag for a blanket, and a hungry three-year-old to feed. She had no job, no property, no belongings. She didn't even have a last name.

"When she got freed up, she chose August as her last name," Mama said. "Most folks went with the last name of their master, but she wouldn't have any of it. She wanted me to remember my daddy, so she put him in our name. Naming's a powerful thing."

I felt the warmth of her arm on my back.

She continued: "That's all I got left of my daddy. No memories, only a name to remind me of the month he left. You be glad you got yourself a real live daddy who loves you to pieces."

I felt sad, thinking of Mama growing up without a daddy.

"So don't you forget—you got August blood in you, the same way you got Thomas blood. Both are good, but different. So when your daddy and Boo Nanny quarrel, I want you to think: I'm the luckiest boy alive. 'Cause I got myself two ways of looking at a thing, not just one."

SEVEN

Once a month, Mama only worked a half day on Saturday and met me and Boo Nanny downtown to shop at the open-air market. Black farmers had stalls at the market, something Daddy said happened in our city but not in other cities.

One early October day, we arranged to meet on a corner across from the streetcar stop, several blocks from the market. Mama worked at one of the big gingerbread mansions along Third Street, less than half a mile away, and she was walking from work.

I was the first one there. The air smelled of fish and manure. It hadn't rained for quite some time, and the waste from the horses and mules had gotten packed into the spaces around the cobbles. While I waited, I looked in the window of the millinery shop at the fancy hats with swooping feathers stuck in the bands. Boo Nanny came up beside me and looked at the display. "Ladies keep buying them hats, we ain't gone have no birds left."

The streetcar approached, spewing white and blue chips of light as the wire skipped over the joints above. With grinding brakes, it stopped and let out the passengers. A white woman with gray hair stepped down. I noticed her because she was wearing a hat with so many feathers, she might as well have shot a snowy egret and stuck it on her head.

The bird killer bunched up her skirt in one hand so it wouldn't sweep the dirty street, then crossed over on the arm of a finely dressed older gentleman who also accompanied a woman Mama's age. They appeared to be headed for the millinery shop. As they passed us, the man stopped and said, "Why, I do believe it's Mammy Jo. Is that you, Josephine?"

"Hello, Colonel. I reckon it be me, all right." The colonel was a tall man with lots of white hair and a huge forehead. He must be smart. Daddy always said that my high forehead was a sign of intelligence.

"Why, it's been"—he did a quick calculation—"thirty-three years!"

"Eighteen sixty-five," I said, showing off my ability to do the math in my head. The older woman gave me a sour look and snapped open her parasol. She wore a white dress and white gloves, as if she were an ancient bride. Her powdered face was so pale, it faded into the white background of her dress, like the sky after you look directly into the sun.

At that moment, Mama caught up to our group. "And this must be your daughter. Your lovely daughter. Sadie, is it?" He gazed at her a long time. Mama looked down and shifted back and forth on her feet as if pushing organ pedals.

The colonel's wife tugged at his elbow and said, "Richard, we need to go."

"In a minute, dear."

The colonel turned to the younger woman with him and said, "When Sadie was a baby and you were four, you used to wheel her around in your wicker baby carriage and pretend to be a mother. One time, the carriage got stuck on the root of a tree. You tried and tried to get it over the bump. You were such a smart thing, I couldn't believe you couldn't figure out how to do it."

The colonel kept staring at Mama. I had always been taught not to stare. I guess the colonel hadn't had three adults nagging him about good manners.

"It's late. We must go." The wife put a gloved hand on the colonel's arm. "I insist."

He turned to me and said, "I can see you're a smart boy." He reached into his pocket and handed me a nickel. "Go get yourself a lemon phosphate."

I couldn't believe my good fortune. "Thank you, sir," I said, clutching the coin in my fist.

But Boo Nanny pried the coin from my hand and returned it to the colonel. "Thank you, but he don't be needing nothing sweet."

After we had parted company, Mama's features were twisted and her eyes narrow. She insisted on going straight home without stopping at the market. I wondered if she was mad at me. I was the one who deserved to be hopping mad. I turned to Boo Nanny. "Why did you tell the colonel I didn't need anything sweet?" I pouted.

"Don't you be showing me that bottom lip."

"But I'm thirsty." I could all but taste the sweetness in my mouth. The only time I got lemon phosphates was when Lewis's father treated.

"The day I accepts charity from the likes of Colonel Allman be the day sweet Jesus turns hisself brown," she said.

The walk home was hot, dusty, and silent. When we got to the kitchen, Mama turned to Boo Nanny and said, "It's true, isn't it?"

Boo Nanny, who was always quick with a comeback, seemed to be without words.

"How could you? Why didn't you tell me? Mama, what you be thinking?"

"They's things in this world you better off not knowing."

"You told me my daddy was sold south."

Boo Nanny straightened her head, the only part of her she could straighten. "My husband was sold south."

"Your husband. What about my daddy?"

"What do it matter? The past be past."

"You lied to me." She ran to her room and slammed the door.

"What's wrong with Mama?" I asked Boo Nanny. Mama never took to her bed in the middle of the day.

"She's had herself a powerful shock."

"What kind of shock?"

"You's too young to be asking such questions."

I knew it had to do with the colonel. "Who was that white man we met downtown?"

"He be the owner of the plantation where I worked." Then she said, as if an afterthought, "He be the owner of me." She put her hands on either side of my face and pulled it level with hers. "Ain't nobody gone claim me or you as they property ever again."

Boo Nanny went to her room and closed the door. I stood in the kitchen, unsure of what to do. I felt completely alone. I didn't realize how much I was used to having noise around me—the happy sounds of scrubbing, chopping, rustling newspaper. Now all was silent.

After a short while, I knocked on Mama's door.
When she didn't answer, I opened it. I rarely went into
my parents' room, and now it felt strange. The windows
were open, and the wind lifted the lace curtains. Mama
had taken off her shoes and lay facedown on the bed-
spread, fully dressed, with her face in the pillow and a
hand gripping one of the rungs of the white iron bed, as
if she were trying to get out of jail.

I stood over her, close, without touching, to see if she
would move. Her skirt was bunched up around her like
an unopened parasol. The stockings on her feet were
bumpy with darning.

"Leave me be. I needs a rest." Her voice was muffled
from the pillow but thick with sniffles.

I wanted to make her laugh or at least smile. I tried to
remember what made her happy. On her birthday, when
I made her something pretty from the forest, she smiled.
When I told jokes Lewis told me, she never laughed,
mainly because I messed them up.

Then I had an idea. I had my very own copy of *Treasure Island* that Daddy had given me for Christmas. I
loved to lose myself in the world of adventure.

"Can I read you a story?" I said.

Without moving her head, she groped the air with
her hand. When she found my arm, she squeezed. I took
that to mean yes.

I got the book from my room and turned to the first page. I knew how the story turned out, for I had read it several times—twice on my own, and once to Boo Nanny—but still I couldn't wait to get into the tale again.

Mama lay quietly, still facedown, as I read aloud. Every so often, she shifted. Once, she was so still I thought she had fallen asleep, and I closed the book, keeping my finger in the place, but a muffled voice said, "Don't stop." And I didn't, until I heard Daddy come in the back door. Then I marked my place and went to meet him.

"Something's bad wrong with Mama. You better go see quick," I said.

He looked startled and went straight to their room. I heard their muffled voices, low and familiar, but I couldn't make out what they were saying.

He stayed a long time. Finally he came out and quietly closed the door. He looked upset.

"Is Mama going to be all right?" I said.

"She's a strong woman. She'll get over it."

"Get over what? Does she have the flu?"

"No, she's got sickness of the heart. You know how, when you eat something that doesn't agree with you, your stomach hurts? Well, it's the same with the heart."

I was alarmed. Mr. Howe down the street had had heart problems and took to his bed and never got up.

"We need to be extra nice to her for the next few days. Since the womenfolk are down, I guess I'll have to rustle up something to eat. I think I can manage breakfast."

Everything else was upside down, so why not breakfast for supper?

Daddy said he could handle any dish that had one ingredient, but he was kidding himself. He burned the bacon. When he cracked the eggs into the bacon grease, bits of the shell broke off into the pan. Our supper that night was gritty eggs and black bacon, but it tasted good to me.

The next day was Sunday, but neither Mama nor Boo Nanny went to church. They barely talked to each other. In the afternoon, when Boo Nanny left to visit neighbors, Mama asked me to come to the parlor. I felt a lecture coming on and wondered what I had done wrong. The night before had been a night of tears and silence, and a mysterious illness that felled the womenfolk but left the men standing. Life was still not back to normal, and things you thought you could count on, you couldn't.

Mama sat down on one end of the horsehair sofa. "Come sit on your mama's lap like you used to," she said.

I wasn't a baby anymore. On the other hand, I wanted

to be nice to Mama because she was so sad. I sat close to her—but not in her lap—and put my head against her shoulder.

It was a hot Indian summer evening, and the whip-poor-wills called to one another across the vacant lot. She put her arm around me and said, "I never told you why we named you Moses."

Mama was not a storyteller—she left that to Boo Nanny. But as she told me the story of how I got my name, I realized I had underestimated her. I listened closely because I knew, deep down, that this was the kind of story you only told once.

Boo Nanny was raised on a coastal turpentine plantation, Mama said. Pinefield was mostly longleaf pine forest and cypress swamp, with salt marsh in a broad band near the ocean. The river by the house fed into the Cape Fear and provided easy transportation to the Wilmington port for the barrels of pitch, tar, and turpentine produced on the plantation.

The Pinefield slaves were known for being highly skilled. There were chippers, pullers, and dippers to get the turpentine from the trees, coopers and carpenters to make barrels, and a wood chopper to fuel the turpentine still. In addition, there were the house slaves—maids, cooks, a laundress, a seamstress, nursemaids, and personal servants.

Boo Nanny—known as Mammy Jo to the Allman family—worked as a laundress and cook.

Three years before Mama was born, and a year before the War Between the States began, Boo Nanny gave birth to a son named Henry. He was a dark baby, like his daddy, who was a field hand.

Boo Nanny kept Henry in a sweetgrass basket beside her in the kitchen, which was a separate building a dozen yards from the Big House. Henry was a chubby, happy baby and rarely cried.

In early October, when he was two and a half months old, a hurricane hit the coast. The old-timers could tell by the way the hens ruffled their feathers and the livestock acted skittish that a storm was coming.

The Big House was built with its back to the ocean. The first- and second-floor porches that spanned the front of the house looked over the river and the vast longleaf pine forests.

Rain beat against the windows, and a frightful wind shook the house. Boo Nanny was putting away laundry in Mistress's room when Colonel Allman came in and told his wife that he needed all the house servants to help collect the turpentine equipment. He had recently made a huge investment in a European method of collecting the sap, using clay jars instead of the more common chop boxes carved into the base of the trees.

"You'd put your human stock at risk to protect some crazy European system? That's insanity," she said.

"I can't afford to lose the new equipment."

"I knew that newfangled system was a mistake."

"What's done is done. I need all hands, except Josephine."

"Why spare her?"

"She has a new baby."

"I'll take care of it," Mistress said.

Colonel Allman sent the men to the edge of the swamp to lash down the big log rafts used to transport the turpentine. They also had to secure the barrels, the distillery, the kiln, and the condensing vats. Boo Nanny was sent with the headman to gather the clay jars that collected the sap as it dripped from gashes in the pine trunks.

She and the other house slaves started out, hand in hand, across the field, but the wind was so strong it scattered them apart. The rain angled down and stung her back like a thrashing with a sweet-gum switch.

Great swirls of wind whipped the treetops. The gushing rain was as powerful as a waterfall. Above the sound came the occasional crash as the wind wrenched the weaker limbs from the trees.

Boo Nanny ran from tree to tree, throwing her arms around the trunks to steady herself in the wind. With her cheek against the trunk, sticky where the chippers had stripped away the bark to let the sap run out, she embraced the tree like a dance partner. When she felt safe, she reached for the clay jar and put it in a handcart under a tarp. She worked in the lonesome darkness, for though others were nearby, she could not see or hear them. Whenever she called out, the wind took her voice and wrapped it into its howl.

After she had worked for several hours in the false night of the storm, light returned to the sky, the rain was spent, the winds died down, and an eerie stillness fell over the forest. The birds and animals kept to themselves, and the only sound was the dripping of water from the trees. She could see, down the wide aisle between the pines, the other slaves working. She looked about at the wreckage of the storm and marveled that she had survived. Soaking wet, her skin numb from the beating rain, she rested her back against a tree and closed her eyes, but the headman, knowing more about storms than she did, moved her forward, saying the wind was only resting and would return, and there were acres and acres of trees remaining.

She didn't believe him, but before long the monster came back, as furious as before.

They worked well into the night. The rain was still falling hard when they returned to the Big House and discovered that the worst was not over. The hurricane had hit at high tide on the day of the full moon. The tidal river, already filled to its highest point, could not hold the rain and swelled over its banks, flooding the barn and the Big House.

The slaves climbed into the barn loft. Hungry, scared, and wet, they spent the night huddled together watching the rising water, a foul-smelling soup filled with dark bobbing objects—a dead chicken, an empty barrel, driftwood. They were kept awake by the whinnying of the horses and the lowing of frightened cows, all sloshing about in water up to their necks. One of the log rafts broke loose and crashed into the side of the barn, creating a big gash. Through the opening, Boo Nanny could see a single kerosene light on the second floor of the Big House, and she felt comforted knowing that her baby was safe in the only dry spot on the plantation.

It was morning before the water level went down enough that Boo Nanny could wade to the Big House. A large log from the raft blocked the back entrance, so she entered by the front door for the first time in her life. The hallway was filled with yapping and barking as Colonel Allman came down the stairs with his prize hunting dogs, which he had herded to the second floor for safety during the flood. He did not seem to mind that she came in the front door—the storm had upended all rules of behavior.

In the dining room, overturned chairs and broken china were scattered about. A fish flapped on the soaked Oriental carpet. A silver tea set and candelabras had been tossed about in the water and landed in odd places. An ugly brown line on the wallpaper indicated that the water had risen waist-high. Mistress stood over the open drawer of the highboy.

"My linens. My beautiful linens!" she wept.

When she saw Boo Nanny, she said, "Where have you been? We have work to do."

"Where's Henry?" Boo Nanny asked.

A look of wildness flashed in Mistress's eyes. Her mouth opened into a large O of horror.

"Where's my baby boy?" Boo Nanny repeated.

Mistress started babbling. "It was madness. Everything happened at once. The wind against the windows. Rain beating down. The water gushed in. Oh, it was terrible. Pure chaos. We ran upstairs."

Boo Nanny didn't wait for her to finish. She broke out running from the house, splashing barefoot through the ankle-deep water.

Evidence of the flood was everywhere. Broken limbs blocked the path. Wind and water had tumbled everything together and rearranged it. A silver tray, tarnished dark purple and copper, had lodged itself in a stand of crape myrtle. The herb garden was a mat of vegetation killed by the salt water. Seaweed, sea oats, straw, and shells were scattered about.

A tree had toppled over and lay on its side, the root-ball above the water. Mats of sea oats had collected against the dam formed by broken branches, overturned trees, driftwood, and stray barrel staves.

Boo Nanny forged forward, the salt water stinging the cuts in her feet from the sandspurs, razor grass, random debris. She climbed over a log and thrashed through the forest, her long skirt torn, the sleeve of her blouse ripped. Swatting at the mosquitoes, clawing at the itching bites on her arms, she swept clear the vines that hung down in her path. She had to find her baby.

She stopped only long enough to smear mud on her bare arms and face to keep away the mosquitoes. She was single-minded. She kept going, a mother's instinct pointing her in the right direction.

Water was everywhere, and even the high ground looked like a swamp. When she reached the bald cypress and tupelo gums, she knew she had entered the true swamp. The wind had stripped the water oaks of much of the gray hanging moss and scattered it about in drifts, like giant rats' nests.

She was deathly afraid of water moccasins and alligators, but this did not stop her. She splashed forward.

Up ahead, she saw the sweetgrass basket, surrounded by reeds and angled against the root-ball of an overturned tree. Her first thought was of Moses in the bulrushes.

"Henry," she cried. "Henreeeeeee!"

With her last bit of energy she broke into a run, splashing, not bothering to find high, dry ground. She tripped on an underwater root, fell, and took in a mouthful of water. She spit it out, coughed, scrambled up, and kept going. She reached the basket, chest heaving. Henry lay there peacefully, his fist curled up against his cheek like a new fern. She chucked him gently under the chin, and his head fell over to the side, limp.

She took the baby out of the basket and clutched him to her chest. He could no longer be scared. He was beyond that. She could scream, wail, and cry to the heavens, to anyone who would listen, and still he would not be scared.

She cradled the limp body in her arms and howled at the sun, which beat so clear and bright on the wet world left behind by the flood. The baby was still gooey, and the mud on his skin mixed with hers.

After she had spent her rage, but before grief set in, she clutched the child to her breast, returned to the Big

House, and marched straight up the main staircase—the second time in her life she had entered by the front door. Dripping mud, she went directly to Mistress's room.

Mistress had taken to her bed with a case of nerves. Boo Nanny didn't say a word, but set Henry on the white lace coverlet. The baby's limbs flopped out, like those of a rag doll. Mud seeped through the lace. Mistress screamed. Colonel Allman came running, along with one of the house servants, who fainted at the sight.

"Get them out of here. My nerves. I can't take it!" Mistress said.

Colonel Allman turned to Boo Nanny and said, "Josephine, please. She didn't mean any harm. You must believe that. I'll pay for the funeral." He covered the baby with lace. "You can take this coverlet. It's a family heirloom."

Boo Nanny took Henry but left the coverlet, knowing in her heart that she would rather bury her child in a clean, threadbare rag of her own.

When the ground dried out, she buried her baby in the slave graveyard. Mistress banned her from the house, and she was confined to the kitchen.

After Mama finished telling me the story, we sat quietly without speaking. In the other room, I could hear Daddy rustling his paper.

"Was that the old white lady we saw downtown yesterday?" I asked, breaking the silence.

She nodded.

"Now I understand why she couldn't wait to leave."

"That be one reason."

"What's the other?"

"You too young to understand."

Sometimes I wanted to be a man, but that night, I wanted to be a boy, so I didn't ask any more questions.

"When you was born," Mama said, "I had a mind to call you Henry, but Boo Nanny said no, you be Moses—a leader. Someone who lives to tell the tale."

EIGHT

The Saturday of my birthday finally arrived, and I awoke to a clear October day, when the trees hadn't even thought about changing and the weather was so hot that you'd never have known it was fall. This was the day I was going to ride the train for the first time. For my birthday, Grandpa Tip had purchased me and Daddy discount tickets to Fayetteville, about seventy-five miles away.

I shined my shoes and took a bath, even though I had taken one two days before. Boo Nanny ironed my Sunday suit, and I was ready to go long before Daddy.

We walked to the station, and the train was waiting on the tracks. "You go on and board. I'm going to check and see if Grandpa is working on this train," he said. "Just start walking toward the back and I'll catch up with you."

The first car was crowded, so I walked to the next one and took an aisle seat toward the middle of the car so Daddy could easily find me. Several businessmen looked up from their newspapers. An older gentleman sat in front of me with his hat in his lap. A couple of Negroes hoisted luggage onto the shiny racks above the seats. Soon nearly every seat was taken. There was a buzz and bustle in the car, and I had the feeling people were looking at me.

Two rows up, a mother sat with her young daughter, who wore a crisp pinafore and high-top shoes that didn't reach the floor. The mother called the conductor over and whispered something in his ear. Afterward, the conductor approached me.

"You'll have to move on, boy," he said.

"My father will be here any minute. He has the tickets," I said, knowing full well I could not sit here without a ticket.

"Very good, but this car is reserved. The colored car is further back. Move along, now."

Heat spread to my ears and I felt searing shame, as if I were being made to stand in the corner with a dunce cap for something I didn't do.

Lewis hadn't told me about this. Daddy and Grandpa hadn't mentioned it, either. I felt betrayed.

At that moment, Daddy came up.

"Come along, Moses. It's not as crowded in back," he said.

We walked until we reached a run-down car that hadn't been swept in quite some time. The windows were so cloudy I couldn't see out. The seats were starting to shed their stuffing, and the water cooler had gnats floating on the surface. Mama would have had a fit if she'd seen this filthy car.

"Why do we have to sit here?" I said.

"It's better. Not as crowded," Daddy said without emotion.

My stomach felt queasy—the car smelled almost as bad as the underground tunnels—and I tried to open a window to get some air, but the latch was stuck. After trying several windows, I found one that worked (it was clearer, too), and we moved to that row. Grandpa Tip was not working on this train. If he were, he would never allow this car to be in such a state.

This was not at all what I had imagined when I dreamed of train travel. But I didn't want to hurt Daddy's feelings, so I tried to hide my disappointment.

Daddy was quiet. After a while, he said, "Come on, give me a smile. When we get moving, it's going to be fun."

"I guess," I said.

When the train chugged out of the station, Daddy

took out his gold watch and flipped open the lid. "Ten-oh-five. Right on time," he said, trying to recapture the excitement.

He gave me the watch to hold. The lid was engraved with the letters *H* and *J* intertwined with a large *T* in the middle, for Herbert Jackson Thomas.

"This is Grandpa Tip's watch. It keeps railroad time, down to the second. It was the most precious object he owned, and he gave it to me when I graduated from Howard University. He didn't want to wait till he met the eleven fifty-nine for me to have the watch."

"The eleven fifty-nine?"

"That's what railroad employees say when someone dies. 'There's no way to escape a ride on the eleven fifty-nine,' Grandpa Tip used to say when I was a boy."

I asked about the tiny dents in the lid. Daddy explained, "When your grandpa bought the watch, he was afraid of getting cheated, so he bit into it to see if it was real gold. The deal was, if the watch turned out to be gold, it was his, teeth marks and all. It was gold, and he kept his end of the bargain."

The train picked up speed as we left the city, and I looked out the window. The tides covered the marsh grass so only the tips showed. "When you graduate from college, the watch will be yours," Daddy said.

"Really?" I felt my heart catch. I held the prized object in the palm of my hand. The ticker throbbed like the heartbeat of a small bird.

The train passed over a high, narrow bridge that crossed the Cape Fear. Below, all I could see was blue streaming beneath me, and I felt the giddy sensation of flying.

When the train arrived in Fayetteville, we were the only ones from our car to get off, but hordes from the other cars streamed off until the station swelled with people shoulder to shoulder, surging toward the exit.

Outside, Daddy said, "Stay close to me. Don't get separated." I was too old to hold his hand and I didn't want to embarrass myself by holding on to the sleeve of his jacket, but I kept close.

In front of the Hotel Lafayette, a parade was forming. Along the length of Main Street, people hung from second-floor windows or lined the parade route. Some had climbed lampposts. They cheered, shouted, and waved handkerchiefs and hats as the brass band set off, followed by a string of carriages. Confederate flags flapped red against the blue sky.

Two uniformed men in blue coats with brass buttons and red trim held up a banner that said DEMOCRATIC PARTY.

"I see now why there were discount tickets," Daddy said. "This was a mistake."

"No, it's great," I said, regaining the enthusiasm I had lost in the train. I loved the color and noise of a parade. It made the day special.

"We need to catch the next train back," Daddy said.

"But it's my birthday," I said.

He hesitated, then said, "Well, it's a pity to pay all that money just to turn around and go back. We'll stay for a while, I guess. But stay close."

We took a parallel street to avoid the crowd.

"What are people celebrating?" I asked.

"It's a Democratic rally. I'll explain later. Don't call attention to yourself. This is not a welcoming group."

Several blocks up, we emerged, and the crowds had thinned out. We stayed back and watched from around the corner as four white horses pulled a fancy float with dozens of young girls in long white dresses waving to the crowd. The banner above them read: WHITE SUPREMACY— PROTECT US.

"Ignorance is an ugly thing to watch in action," Daddy muttered.

A group of Rough Riders fresh from the Spanish-American War marched by. I recognized them because a black infantryman, One-Armed Pete, wandered around our neighborhood in uniform, chattering to himself, as if it were his head and not his arm that he left behind on San Juan Hill.

Next came more carriages carrying Democratic dignitaries from surrounding cities and counties.

"Well, if it isn't old Waddell," Daddy said as a carriage passed by, surrounded by a walking group from the White Government Union.

"You know him?"

"He's my nemesis. Politically speaking."

Challenge word. I cocked my head, and Daddy explained, "A rival."

I did what I always did with a new word—worked it around in my head so it would stick. I ticked off the people I could count as a nemesis. Johnny, the spoiled rich boy who was now Lewis's best friend, was a nemesis. Tommy used to be my nemesis, when he and his pals controlled one side of the railroad tracks. But once I got to know him, he became my friend. A nemesis could be converted to a friend if you knew enough about him.

There was a lag in the parade and I thought the festivities were over, but the spectators stayed in place. Then, in a cloud of dust, hundreds of men thundered by on horseback giving rebel yells. They all wore red shirts and carried Winchesters, shotguns, and pistols. A few shot into the air. It was a scary sight. The crowd cheered as the men galloped to the fairground.

"Who are they?" I asked.

"I don't know. Ruffians of some sort." Daddy scowled and bit his lower lip. "I want to find out more."

Daddy held on to my arm, and we fell in behind the horde of people following the parade route.

At the fairground, people streamed in from all directions in buggies and wagons, on foot and on bicycles. The air was thick with the smell of smoke from the pits, where several pigs, strung up by their feet, were being smoked.

Everyone was in a holiday spirit, like our Memorial Day celebration, but I didn't share the mood. Much as Daddy spoke highly of white people, I knew that most people here wouldn't care one bit if our entire race caught the 11:59. When I turned around to ask Daddy if we could leave, he was gone. He had been right behind me seconds before. He shouldn't be hard to find. His was the only other dark face in the crowd. I looked in every direction. People swirled around me, heading for the free food.

"What are you doing?" said a woman holding an unopened parasol.

"Looking for my daddy," I said.

"I'm sure he's not at this gathering. Move along, now. This is no place for you," she said, and tapped me on the back of my legs with the parasol.

I wandered around the crowd with a growing sense of unease. The sun beat down. People ate and drank and mingled. I couldn't find Daddy anywhere.

After an hour or so, my feet hurt and I was hungry. I stopped by a long plank table beneath a banner that said FREE BARBEQUE. ALL WELCOME.

By this time, hundreds had gotten there before me, and the table was covered with shredded cabbage and pools of vinegar from the spilled slaw.

An assembly line of women in sleeveless aprons that buttoned down the back produced mountains of barbeque sandwiches. Some women dropped balls of cornmeal into a huge vat of spitting oil. My mouth watered. I grabbed a sandwich and some fried cornmeal and was starting to leave when I heard one of the matrons shout, "Thief! Stop him!"

I looked around to see who the culprit was. When someone cried "There he is!" I realized that they were talking about me, and I darted through the crowd.

When I got to a group of men in red shirts, I crouched down as if hiding in the marsh grass. My heart beat faster as I saw several men making their way through the crowd after me.

I waddled like a duck to a tree that spread its branches over a table with a barrel on top. The horseback brigade crowded around. They wore all manner of different shirts—silk, cotton, broadcloth. The only thing the shirts had in common was the color red.

I dropped my sandwich, then tried to climb the tree

but my shoes slipped on the trunk, so I took them off, along with my socks and Sunday jacket, and scooted up the tree barefoot. I had a great view of the crowd, but I didn't see Daddy anywhere.

The men beneath the tree laughed and joked loudly; a few men broke into song. At the table, one man pushed another aside so he could fill his glass from the barrel, and a scuffle broke out. I was careful not to make any noise in the tree. I didn't want anyone to know I was there.

From my perch I could see the men in suits standing on a stage wrapped in red, white, and blue bunting. They all carried pitchforks. The main speaker was introduced: Pitchfork Ben Tillman, from South Carolina. He wore a patch over his eye, like a pirate. This caught my interest. Maybe he was swashbuckling and courageous like my favorite pirate, Blackbeard, though pitchforks were not commonly associated with pirates.

Climbing higher for a better view, I straddled a branch of the tree. The pirate was a fiery speaker. He shouted until his face turned red and his one eye bulged. The black patch seemed to be the only thing keeping his other eye from popping out into the crowd.

The drunken men below me made such a commotion that I could only pick up bits and pieces of the oratory, but when I heard my hometown mentioned, I paid closer attention.

"Look at these beautiful young ladies in the audience, the blossom of Southern maidenhood—our pride and our most cherished possession," said the pirate. "The scurrilous article written by the black editor in Wilmington was an insult to the women of North Carolina!"

Men behind him on the stage stabbed their pitchforks in the air. I got a prickly feeling on the back of my neck. Then the speaker—I had already demoted him from being a pirate—shouted, "That Negro ought now to be food for catfish in the bottom of the Cape Fear River instead of going around aboveground! Send him to South Carolina and let him publish any such offensive stuff, and he will be killed."

The man ended his speech with a rousing call to action, his voice cracking from the exertion: "Will you save the great state of North Carolina from Fusionism and Negro domination?"

"Yes, we will!" came the roaring response. Men on stage raised their pitchforks to the sky.

"Restore security to the white women of the state?" the orator said.

"Yes, we will!" the crowd shouted. Men in the audience held up their hats. Confederate flags waved from every corner.

"Protect our fireside and loved ones?"

"Yes, we will!" came the answer a thousand strong. Somewhere in the distance, a cannon went off.

"Save jobs for our hardworking Anglo-Saxon brethren?"

"Yes, we will!" The roar was deafening.

"Let every patriot rally to the white man's party. To your tents, O Israel!"

With that, the one-eyed man finished and wild clapping broke out. He waved and basked in the adoration of the crowd. Each time he tried to leave, more applause brought him back. A man on stage passed him a pitchfork, and he raised the tool like a spear in triumph. Finally, after the crowd had exhausted itself and the cheers petered out, there was a lull as people waited for the next speaker. I looked out into the crowd and spied Daddy at the edge, his head moving right and left in sharp, quick movements, like a squirrel.

I was torn. If I shouted out to him, I'd call attention to myself. But if he didn't happen to look up, he wouldn't see me, and I might lose him for good. So I cried out, "Daddy! Daddy, up here!"

Several men below looked up into the branches.

One of the red-shirted men said, "Lookee there. Somebody done treed a coon."

This set off drunken laughter and merriment.

"What say we have him for dinner," came a voice from the crowd.

Someone fired a shot into the air, shredding leaves not far from my perch. I was too terrified to move.

Daddy made his way through the throng, frantically moving people aside to get to the tree.

"That darkie pushed me," one man said.

Suddenly a mob of red-shirted men surrounded Daddy. Beneath me I saw a vast circle of red with black at its center, like a poppy.

Daddy looked dignified, with his wireless glasses and coat and tie still in place after an afternoon in the hot sun. The other men looked messy, with shirts untucked and pant legs half in, half out of their boots. Everyone except Daddy carried a gun.

"Ain't no nigger lays a hand on one of ourn," said another man. Sweat stains had turned his shirt a deep maroon under the arms.

I needed to do something—anything—to distract them, and I needed to do it fast. I shimmied down to a lower limb, swung down, and gave the barrel a solid kick. It overturned and clear liquid washed over the table and dripped off the edge.

"What the hell . . ." Men made a rush for the table and thrust their glasses under the edge to catch the drips.

Daddy yelled, "Station!" I dropped to the ground and took off running, barefoot, and didn't stop until I had reached the edge of the fairground.

Steering clear of Main Street, I took a parallel road to the train station and sat on a bench on the colored side, grateful for the shabby security of separate waiting rooms.

Daddy arrived not long after, out of breath. When he saw me, he hugged me tight. I was still shaking.

"I've been frantic. Don't ever do that again," he said. Up close, he felt damp.

"I didn't mean to," I said, and felt calmer as he squeezed the shivers clear out of me.

"I was worried to death," he said.

He didn't let go for a long time. When he did, he looked down at my bare feet.

"I'm sorry," I said. I had lost my jacket and my only good pair of shoes, and my Sunday pants were in tatters. I was going to catch it from Mama when I got back home. The only plus was that without anything to wear, I might be able to avoid Sunday school.

"It doesn't matter one bit," he said. "You're safe and that's all that counts." He hugged me again.

"Who were those men in red shirts?" I said when he let go.

"I asked around. They're called—no surprise—Red Shirts. It's a Klan-like organization out of South Carolina, and as far as I can tell, their sole purpose is to terrorize people before the elections. If you ever see them in Wilmington, I want you to stay as far away as you can."

He explained the political situation to me, and I did my best to follow. Lewis and me against Tommy and his gang I understood, but when more than two sides were involved, I lost track. It made me feel good, though, that Daddy talked to me as an adult.

He said that the Republicans, Lincoln's party and the one preferred by most Negroes, had joined forces with the Populists and farmers to form the Fusion party, which now controlled the state legislature and the governor's office. The Democrats vowed to win the power back in this election. Their white supremacy campaign was whipping up fear of Negro domination, particularly in the eastern part of the state, where blacks outnumbered whites.

"The Democrats have whites thinking that we black folk will steal their jobs, harm their women, and ruin their lives. If people are afraid, they'll do anything."

"Why do they hate us, Daddy?"

"Ignorance. People hate and fear what they don't understand. The best thing we can do is get to know our white neighbor, work with him, show him what makes us tick—that we're no different from him."

"But we *are* different, aren't we?" I asked. "We have dark skin."

"White and black are natural attributes. Crows aren't black because they dip themselves in ink every day.

Seagulls don't become white because they wash themselves every day. Black and white are an integral part of who they are. That doesn't mean one is better than the other."

"Aren't white people better than us?" I asked.

"Not better. Different. Everybody is an individual. It's like hair. Some people have red hair, some brown, some blond. But that doesn't mean we're different inside."

People with red hair didn't have to sit in dirty train cars, I thought but did not say. I wondered if editing what you said was part of growing up.

What I did say was "I don't think the Red Shirts would agree with you."

"You've heard the saying 'Every crow thinks her own bird the fairest'? It's common to find one's own kind the most beautiful. From the seagull's perspective, white is more natural and beautiful. The opposite is true for crows. Who's to say white is more beautiful than black? Who sets the standard?"

"I've seen crows and seagulls fighting over scraps at the wharf," I said.

"That's why we need good government—to make sure things are equal, to counteract man's tendency to grab the spoils for his own kind and cut out the others. Look at Wilmington. Blacks and whites work closely together on the Board of Aldermen."

Suddenly I felt scared for Daddy. Was he up for re-election? When I asked him, he said, "Not until next year. The upcoming election is for state and county officials. The campaign's going to be far dirtier than I imagined. But I refuse to be dragged down to their level of hatred and half-truths. It's not dignified."

I trusted Daddy. He was the smartest person I knew. But given what I'd seen that day, I wondered if this might be one instance where Boo Nanny was more on the mark when she said, "Trust white folks if you wants, but might as well put you hand in a pit of vipers."

The train arrived. I had been humiliated by having to ride in the colored car on the way to Fayetteville, but on the way home, I was mighty glad to have our own car, dirty and smelly though it was. I certainly wouldn't forget this birthday. It confirmed what I had been feeling in the days leading up to my birthday: I didn't want to grow up.

NINE

A dark-skinned man stood on a crate giving a speech in the middle of our street one hot Indian summer day in late October. I recognized Crazy Drake, a harmless neighbor who cycled in and out of the Negro loony bin in Goldsboro. When he wasn't speechifying, he goose-stepped around the neighborhood with a stick for a rifle. Today he was dressed in a beaver hat with a bushy tail down the back. Around his neck he wore a handwritten cardboard sign like the ones children wore at school that said DUNCE. Perhaps that was what his *should* have said, but his sign said MAYOR.

From around the corner, I heard the fish man chanting, "Bring out de dishpan. Here come de fish man." The children playing nearby crowded around the fish man's cart to watch the crabs jump up and click their claws. This left Crazy Drake speaking to an empty street.

His voice rose and fell in the cadence of the best Negro preachers, but as Daddy and I got closer, I realized he was talking gibberish. Like people speaking in tongues, he used many recognizable words, but sentence by sentence, the words made no sense.

"Hello, Drake. How are you this fine day?" Daddy said. We were walking the ward to encourage people to vote.

"Right pert, suh."

"You must be awfully hot in that hat."

"This be my good-luck hat. You voting for me, suh?"

"I'm certainly going to the polls on November eighth, and hope you will, too."

"I aim to, suh." He tipped his fur hat and then returned to his oratory.

After we got down the street out of earshot, I said, "Can Crazy Drake vote?"

"Son, please don't call him that. Labels blind us to our common interests."

Nobody in the neighborhood would know who I was talking about if I referred to plain old Drake. I didn't even know if that was his first or last name.

"But he's crazy."

"He hasn't had the advantages you have. Never judge a man till you've walked a mile in his shoes."

Crazy Drake, I noticed, wore no shoes. His toenails were pitted and yellow, like jingle shells.

"Can he vote?" I asked.

"You have to be male, of age, registered, and an American citizen, but otherwise, anyone can vote."

"Even if they're daft?" I said.

"Sanity is not a requirement." This set off a lecture about his cherished democracy. It didn't take much to get him going. "What if people decided you couldn't vote because you were poor or uneducated? Before you know it, democracy's at stake."

I wondered if Crazy Drake—I mean, *Drake*—could read and write. Was he the one who had penned MAYOR on the sign around his neck?

Daddy continued: "I proposed to the aldermen that we purchase Drake some shoemaker's tools so he could make a living and stay out of trouble, but I couldn't drum up any support for giving money to a crazy Negro when there are so many white people looking for work."

"So the aldermen call him crazy, too," I said, testing the waters for a challenge. Lately I had started to question Daddy and not just take everything he said as the gospel truth.

"That proves my point," he said. "They couldn't see how they would benefit if Drake had a trade that kept him off the street. Common interest."

Daddy and I started canvassing on Fourth Street. I tagged along with him for a while to see how it was done.

We knocked on several doors where no one was home. One woman scolded us for working on the Sabbath and slammed the door in our faces.

At one house we found an older man at home. When he shuffled to the door with a cane, Daddy introduced himself and encouraged the man to support the Republican ticket.

"Why Republican?" the grizzled old man said.

"It's the party of Lincoln, the party that freed you and gave you the vote. You can return the favor by keeping them in power."

Next door we found a man digging a hole in his yard. When Daddy asked if he was going to vote, the man leaned against the shovel and said, "I ain't aimin' to fool with it myself. No siree. You stick yo' finger in the fire, you shore to git burned."

"A vote is the strongest right a citizen has. If we don't exercise that right, we'll never have a voice," Daddy said, but the man remained unconvinced.

The man three houses down said, "I don't do no voting, no suh! That ain't nothin' but trouble. I show up to there, they shoot me fo' true."

"All this talk about violence—it's rumor," Daddy said. "The Democrats are trying their best to scare us away from the polls. You don't have to worry. Your right to vote is protected by the Constitution."

"The Constitution don't mean nothing when I be laying there, cemetery-dead."

I was nervous about going out on my own, but Daddy said we could cover more territory if we worked opposite sides of the street.

I did the best I could, though by nature I was shy and didn't like to talk to strangers. Several men were convinced they would lose their jobs if they showed up at the polls. Why would they believe a twelve-year-old boy who assured them that this was not the case?

After three hours of canvassing, I could think of only one, possibly two men who would go to the polls because of my efforts. I felt discouraged.

"Democracy is hard work," Daddy said, putting his arm around my shoulder. "But it's what makes our country great." He was a proud citizen and never had any doubts. Around me, at least.

But one evening not long afterward, I was on the back porch collecting kindling and he didn't know I was there. Through the window I saw him come into the kitchen and slam the white people's newspaper on the table, opened to the editorial page.

"Drat, if they aren't trying to rile everyone up," he said.

"What's wrong?" Mama said.

"They're reprinting Alex Manly's editorial in the

Messenger every day, with commentary. Listen to this. . . ."

He sat down and read from the paper: "'Every white man in the state having any regard for the purity of his mother, sisters, and daughters must take this matter into consideration,'" he said.

Mama stood behind him and put her hands on his shoulders. "You is all worked up. That's what I loves about you."

He squeezed her hand. "I'm worried, Sadie. I don't know how things are going to end. This is the third day they've reprinted that wretched editorial—always under some slanderous headline like 'Vile and Villainous' or 'An Insult to the White Women of North Carolina.'"

They stopped abruptly when I entered the room with an armful of wood. "What are you talking about?" I asked.

"Shoo, now. We gots adult talk going on here," Mama said.

This caught my attention. Anything she didn't want me to hear was guaranteed to be something really interesting.

But Mama sat down at the organ and Daddy buried himself behind the newspaper, and I didn't hear anything more.

• • •

November's weather was wishy-washy—neither winter nor fall, but something in between. An early frost turned the grass brown, but many days were still warm. In the swamps, the bald cypress trees, worthy of their name, had shed their needles, and their bare branches were bearded with moss. The pin oaks held tight to their leaves, but the crape myrtle and dogwoods cast their yellow and red leaves onto the sand. By this time of year, the songbirds were mostly silent, but wild ducks filled the marshes with their noise.

One afternoon, Lewis rode his bike to my house. I had not seen much of him since school started, so I was excited when he said, "Come, quick. You're not going to believe this!" I jumped on the crossbar and he pedaled us to the armory, a boxy marble building that was home to the Wilmington Light Infantry. We stood on the low stone wall and looked over the wrought-iron fence.

"There it is. See it?" Lewis pointed to an enormous gun with ten barrels, mounted on two wagon wheels. It was not as fat as a cannon, but just as long.

A couple of men in red shirts were hitching the gun up to a horse.

"That's the biggest gun I've ever seen. I'd heard about it, but never seen one. It's a Gatling gun," Lewis said.

The horse and driver started pulling the gun toward Market Street, followed by two Red Shirts on horseback.

"Let's follow," Lewis said.

"Daddy told me to steer clear of the Red Shirts," I said, and wished I'd kept my big fat mouth shut.

"Don't be such a sissy," he said.

We had been together less than half an hour, and already we were falling into old habits. I thought of *Treasure Island*. What would Jim Hawkins do? He would not back down from a Gatling gun. I was sure of it.

I sat on the crossbar, and we followed the Red Shirts at a distance. The shanks of the bay bobbed up and down as it trotted along, pulling the gun, with its ten barrels pointed toward us.

"Maybe they'll fire it! Rat-a-tat-tat-tat-tat," Lewis said, taking both hands off the handlebars and making a shooting motion in the air. I grabbed the bars to hold the wheel straight. Sissy or no, I didn't want to end up in the ditch.

"Can you believe the size of that thing?" Lewis said, and returned to steering.

When we crossed over the bridge where Tommy and his gang had faced off against us, we were in the colored section of town. Neighbors who saw the gun screamed and ran inside. We were traveling on the same streets I had canvassed with Daddy, and I thought of all the men who were afraid to go to the polls. What would they think now?

"Lewis, I want to go home."

Just to needle me, he pedaled faster and pulled up beside the gun.

"Hey, mister, how does that thing work?"

"Runs eight hundred rounds a minute. They used it at San Juan Hill," one of the Red Shirts said.

"What are you going to use it for now?" Lewis asked.

"What's with the questions, Sambo? Now scat."

The two men on horseback closed ranks around the gun, as if to protect it, and we slowed down, putting distance between us and them.

That night at supper, I told my family about the Gatling gun. They looked concerned.

"I hear white folk is organizing block by block, military style," Mama said. "They convinced our people gone torch the town."

"Where did you hear that?" Daddy said.

"The Gilchrists talk."

"Around a Negro?" Daddy said.

"Jackson, to these folk, I be the same color as that windowpane there. 'Cause long as the stew gets on the table and the dishes be cleared, I might as well be invisible."

"White folk is arming theyself to the teef," Boo Nanny said. "That's what I heared at Walker's Grocery."

"We have to be careful not to do anything that will

allow the civic leaders to blame the Negroes if there's trouble. As long as we are quiet, orderly, and submissive to authority, and return home directly after voting, we'll get through this election. Then, when passions cool, we can work on repairing some of the damage," Daddy said.

"Is you going to vote?" Boo Nanny asked.

"Of course. It's the most important thing I do as a citizen. Negroes form a majority in Wilmington. If everyone votes, we will win. It's simple arithmetic."

"I may be an unlettered old crow, but I knows the massa's math," she said.

"Our white friends in the Fusion party have a mutual interest in working with us," Daddy said.

"You so-called white friends, they uses you till they don't need you no mo', then they toss you out quicker than three-day-old fish 'cause you stink and the only fixin' it is to bury you."

I hated it when Boo Nanny and Daddy argued. It was as if the election was tearing everyone apart in the worst way—from the inside out.

With less than a week to go before the election, fear was everywhere. You could feel it in the empty porches, the curtains drawn in the front windows, the deserted streets. Men and women on the way to work kept their eyes down and walked swiftly past the Red Shirts who stalked our neighborhood on foot, on mules, and on horseback, waving their weapons. One rowdy man on patrol shoved Crazy Drake off his soapbox with the butt end of his rifle. When Drake took a wild swing at him with his stick, the Red Shirt chased him down the street on horseback, laughing as the barefoot man whimpered and cowered by a stump like a wounded animal.

These days, wild persimmons hung in the bare branches, ripe for picking. But children were not up in the tree limbs, and women were not passing persimmon pudding over the fence to share with neighbors. Everyone stayed inside, waiting, expecting something awful to happen.

Daddy instructed me to come straight home from school and to avoid crowds of any kind until after the election. But one afternoon I saw a group of white men gathered in front of Thalian Hall, and curiosity got the better of me. I knew Daddy wouldn't have approved, but I needed to test my independence.

I crept along the stone wall and slipped down into one of the basement window wells. From there, no one could see me, but I had a clear view of the man standing at the top of the steps between two massive columns. He was thin and had shaggy eyebrows and a full silver beard that glinted in the sun. I recognized him but couldn't remember his name. It was Daddy's nemesis, the one we had seen in the parade in Fayetteville. Today he wore a suit and tie and looked like a refined gentleman, but when he spoke, he looked crazier than Crazy Drake. Spit spewed from his mouth and his face turned red as he shouted, "You are Anglo-Saxons! You are armed and prepared, and you will do your duty. Be ready at a moment's notice. If you find the Negro out voting, tell him to leave the polls, and if he refuses, kill him, shoot him down in his tracks. We shall win this election, even if we have to do it with guns."

What I heard next I wished I could boast of to my friends and family, but then I would have had to admit that I had been there. News of the speech raced through Darktown, but I was not the source, nor had I seen anyone of my race at the speech. Still, everyone talked about it. Unlike most stories that changed in the retelling, in this story everyone repeated more or less the same quote, either because the horror of it was imprinted on their memories, or because there was no way to make it worse than it already was. What I heard at the end of the bearded man's speech made my heart close up and harden like a clamshell. "We will never surrender to a ragged raffle of Negroes, even if we have to choke the Cape Fear River with carcasses," he said.

Now that my parents wouldn't let me play in the streets or go to Lewis's house, I was bored and lonely. I didn't have brothers or sisters like most people I knew. I needed a companion.

"Can I get a dog?" I asked at the supper table.

"I ain't getting myself one more blessed mouth to feed or take care of," Mama said.

"I'll take care of it," I said.

"You says you will, but if you forgets, am I gone let that poor beast starve?"

"I promise," I said.

"White man promises," muttered Boo Nanny.

"Please." I had already picked out a name for the dog—Jim, after the boy in *Treasure Island*. I didn't care what kind of dog it was, but I wanted it to be brave and adventurous.

"Daddy?" I said, appealing to him. I knew he could overrule the women if he wanted to.

"Listen to your mother," he said.

By Saturday, I thought I might go crazy if I had to spend one more day inside alone. I got Boo Nanny's permission to visit Daddy at work, provided I stayed off the main roads.

The new offices for the *Record* occupied the second floor of a two-story clapboard building near the corner of Seventh and Church, about a mile from the house. The first floor housed the Love and Charity Benevolent Society, a group of colored ladies devoted to raising money to build a Negro wing at the hospital. Whenever I stopped by to see Daddy, they offered me cookies and a pat on the head. I didn't know any of their names, but I called them the Love Ladies.

The newspaper office was a big, open room, with desks at one end and the press at the other. Mr. Manly sat at the desk beside Daddy's, looking at a mock-up of the paper.

While I waited for Daddy to return from reporting, I sat in his chair and stared at the typewriter, with its high black back and dozens of moving parts.

Mr. Manly looked up from his work and said, "Are you going to be a writer like your daddy?"

One thing I never wanted to be was a writer. Not after the bicycle contest. But Mr. Manly was an important man and I didn't want to be impolite, so I said, "I don't know."

"Let me show you how that works," he said. He rolled a blank sheet of paper into the cylinder and typed out the letters of my name, as quickly as someone drumming his fingers on a desk. When he pulled the silver lever, a bell sounded, and I jumped slightly.

"Does this make you a better writer?" I asked.

He smiled kindly. "No, but it's faster, and that's important in the newspaper business. Now you practice. I'll be here if you need help."

I stabbed at a key, and a long metal arm jumped up and slapped a letter against the page. I tried another. It was thrilling.

Before long, a tall white man in a clerical collar approached Mr. Manly. After they greeted each other, he said, "We go a long way back, Mr. Manly. Some of my congregants are convinced there's a vast Negro uprising brewing. Is there any truth to that?"

I typed slower so I could hear.

"Reverend, I can assure you unequivocally that there's no organized uprising," Mr. Manly said. "We're the eyes and ears of the community here at the paper, and if anything were happening, we'd know. Our people can't even buy guns—the white store owners won't sell us ammunition. A few men have rusty muskets or hunting rifles, but you've been out on the streets. We're up against organized militias and heavily armed Red Shirts. Our Negro citizens are terrified. They're afraid to go to the polls."

"I wanted your assurances before saying what I've come here to say. Mr. Manly, you need to get out of town. Today. Right this moment. Angry men are assembling at the armory as we speak. There's talk of justice, and you know what that means."

"I'll go home and pack my things," he said.

"No. There's no time. You have to leave now."

"Shouldn't we wait until after dark?" Mr. Manly said. He was shaking.

"I suggest you leave in broad daylight, when they least expect it. You look as white as any man. It will be easy for you to pass."

"But Red Shirts are posted at every waterway and roadway out of the city."

"I know. We just need a place for you to hide until I can find someone who will give me the Red Shirts' password."

Mr. Manly suggested several hiding places, all of which were rejected by the reverend as too obvious.

"What about your church?" Mr. Manly said.

"My hand can't be seen in this. I hope you understand. I have to strike a balance between being true to my convictions and keeping my job. But there is a young seminary student working for me—Curtis Hanson. He's from Boston and holds the same views I do. We can trust him. For the moment, though, we need a hiding place."

I was tired of being the timid one, the weakling who was forced to take the rebels' side when playing war. I wanted to be brave, the way I had felt underground with Tommy. "I know somewhere no one will look," I piped up.

They both turned to me. "That's Jack Thomas's boy," Mr. Manly said.

I told them about the tunnel.

"That just might work," the reverend said, impressed.

"I also know a back way out of town, if we can get past the sawmill."

"Tell us," the reverend said.

"It's hard to describe. But I can show you. I go that way with my grandmother to look for plants."

Together we made a plan. The reverend would take us to the tunnel entrance and park the carriage there until Mr. Manly was safely underground. Then I would go with the reverend to the Episcopal church and wait in the office. As soon as the reverend was able to find out the password, the seminary student would use the rectory's carriage to drive us to the train station north of town.

On the way to the tunnel, Mr. Manly said very little. I could tell he was nervous. When we reached the entrance, the reverend stayed in the carriage while I went to work. The manhole cover was too heavy to handle alone, so Mr. Manly helped me roll aside the cast-iron disk.

A group of stevedores walked by, and the reverend distracted them with idle chatter. After they turned the corner and disappeared, I scooted down the ladder with the lantern I had taken from the *Record* offices. Mr.

Manly followed. The curved brick ceiling was wet and gleaming. It was close to high tide, judging from the amount of water in the stream. The tunnel reeked of fish and human waste. I set a crate beside the stream among the shells, fish skeletons, and chunks of brick. Mr. Manly made quite a picture, sitting there in his derby hat, suit, cuff links, and silk pocket handkerchief. The smelly sludge reached up over the soles of his shoes.

I remembered well the terror I had felt in the absolute blackness of the tunnel, not knowing if Tommy and I would get out. How odd that now the tunnel felt like the safest place in town.

With the reverend's help, I replaced the manhole cover. We left Mr. Manly behind and went to the Episcopal church, where I was introduced to Curtis Hanson, a young man with skin the color of a peeled banana. He looked sickly, in dire need of one of Boo Nanny's remedies.

I waited in his book-lined office. On one wall was a framed picture of an angel with long, curly blond hair, playing a trumpet of some sort. The angel's eyes were the same color as the flowering vine with heart-shaped leaves that covered our back fence. The bright blue flowers opened in the morning and closed in the afternoon. Boo Nanny called the flower Angel Eyes.

"Do angels have blue eyes?" I once asked her when I was quite a bit younger.

"Angels is just like people," she said. "Some's got theyselves blue eyes, some brown like me and you, some green."

"But what color are angels? Their skin?"

"Angels is like they eyes—every color you could name."

"Then why are the ones in the paintings at church always white?" I asked. Not to needle her—I truly wanted to know. It was a question I'd spent a fair amount of time trying to puzzle out.

Boo Nanny, acting like it was my dedicated mission to aggravate her, said, "You worry me to death with you questions, chile." I never got an answer.

Now I considered asking Mr. Hanson, but I was too shy, and he was busy at his desk, writing. So I kept quiet and tried to find a book to read. There were no adventure stories on the shelf—only books about religion and philosophy. I pulled out a Bible, wondering how one book could be the source of such different reactions in Daddy and Boo Nanny.

Two hours passed, and I was beginning to think the reverend had forgotten us. The whole project was taking more time than I thought. It occurred to me that my family might be worried, but I couldn't back out now. I thought of Mr. Manly waiting in that stinky tunnel, with the ceiling weeping brown tears onto his derby hat. I wished I had thought to bring an umbrella from the office.

At last the reverend returned, successful in his efforts to get the password.

"It's Dog Wing," he said.

"Dog Wing?" Mr. Hanson said, verifying. "That doesn't make sense."

"Exactly. That's what makes it a good password. It's not a phrase someone could guess," the reverend said.

It was late afternoon by the time the seminary student and I returned to collect Mr. Manly, who emerged from the tunnel shaken and damp. He rubbed his shoes in the grass to remove the slime, and then climbed into the front seat of the carriage. I rode in the back. We headed to the north edge of town.

Mr. Hanson held the reins in his quaking hands. Mr. Manly sat on his fingers and stiffened his arms to stop the trembling. It was so strange to watch the most famous man I knew shaking like a wet dog in a cold sack.

Even the horse acted skittish.

I was surprised by the number of men who were patrolling the streets with weapons. A stranger might think the city was at war. The men gathered around tar barrels at the corners and loitered in parks and medians. They did not look particularly prosperous or organized. Some wore tattered civilian clothes, others fragments of Rough Rider uniforms, Confederate grays, or the new outfit of choice, a red shirt. The White Government Union warriors wore white armbands. Many men were drinking. The aldermen had passed an ordinance outlawing alcohol within five days of the election, but there was no one to enforce it.

I remembered what Daddy had told me about the importance of the rule of law when I got caught skinny-dipping. He asked me to imagine what it would be like on the river if everybody made up his own rules, and I immediately pictured ships crashing into one another, masts crisscrossing, bodies going overboard. "Laws help keep order for public safety," he had said. But today, just three days before the election, the city had been taken over by lawless bands of men. Where was the government now? I wondered.

We were out in the open, protected only by Mr. Manly's light skin. To succeed, we had to fool every white man we passed. I clenched my buttocks in fear as we drove by several groups without incident, and the sense of dread kept growing. This caper was not quite the swashbuckling fun I had imagined.

Several blocks ahead, a cluster of men in civilian clothes and carrying rifles blocked the road.

"Uh-oh," Mr. Hanson said under his breath.

A bleat arose from Mr. Manly's throat. Embarrassed, he covered his mouth with a fist and cleared his throat loudly.

"What time is it?" Mr. Hanson asked.

Mr. Manly fumbled in his watch pocket and, after several tries, pulled out his watch—gold like Grandpa Tip's, but without the teeth marks. He tried to open it, but his fingers weren't working properly. I leaned forward in the seat and pressed the button that snapped open the lid. It was already 4:15, and the last train of the day was leaving from the station north of town in twenty-five minutes.

The man in the road held up his hand and shouted, "Halt!"

We did, and my heart skidded like a stone thrown sideways over water.

"Where are you gentlemen going?" the burly, unshaven man asked.

"Up north to buy horses. There's an auction there," Mr. Hanson said. His voice sounded remarkably casual, given the shaking of his hands.

"So late in the day?" the man said. He smelled of tobacco and leather.

"It's tomorrow morning," the seminary student said. "We want to be there first thing."

"Well, we're going to a necktie party for that scoundrel nigger editor," one of the men said. "That oak tree by Morton's Grocery is begging for action."

"I'll leave you to your business," Mr. Hanson said.

He tipped his hat and shook the reins, and the horse picked up its pace.

Mr. Hanson grimly set his jaw, and we continued on in silence. The sawmill was just up ahead, but before we could get there, a group of Red Shirts signaled for the carriage to pull over. I was certain that the loud pounding in my chest could be heard by the coarse man with bad breath and yellow teeth who approached the carriage with another man. Yellow was a color I was starting to associate with white people.

"Evening, sir," Mr. Hanson said. Fear crawled down my chest, restricting my breathing. Half a dozen Red Shirts stayed back by the tar barrel, passing around a jug.

"Howdy, Reverend," the lead man said, fingering the trigger on his rifle.

They exchanged pleasantries. *Hurry*, I thought. *Hurry and let's get out of here.* I didn't have a watch, but I knew time was short. Mr. Hanson must have been thinking the same thing, for he said, "We'd best be on our way."

"If you'd be so kind as to give us the password, we'll let you through."

"Certainly. It's, it's . . ."

In his nervousness, he had forgotten.

Terror squeezed my throat and prevented speech, but I could make primitive sounds. From the backseat, I growled. When Mr. Hanson and the two Red Shirts turned to look at me, I flapped my elbows like a chicken and started yapping like a little fice dog. A look of recognition passed over Mr. Hanson's face.

"What's with the crazy coon?" the lead Red Shirt said.

"Don't worry, our houseboy's a bit simple in the head, but he's harmless," Mr. Hanson said. For a religious man, he was quick with a fib.

"What were you asking?" Mr. Hanson said. "Yes, the password. It's Dog Wing." He pronounced each word distinctly and slipped me a look by way of thanks. I felt proud that my pantomime had helped, and my heartbeat settled down a bit.

"Very well." The Red Shirt turned to Mr. Manly. "And you. How are you?"

Mr. Manly tipped his hat and said, "Fine, thank you, sir."

"He talks funny," the other Red Shirt said.

I felt my insides seize up again. It was over. Mr. Manly's voice had given him away. He looked white, but he sounded black. A crow in seagull feathers.

Mr. Hanson was quick with a response. "I'm from Boston. People down here tell me I have a funny accent." He might have been pale, but he was resourceful.

"You're one of them damn Yankees," the Red Shirt said with suspicion. There was a moment of tense silence, broken by the sound of spit as he sent a squirt of brown tobacco juice onto the shell road. My thoughts bumped into each other in wild confusion as I realized that our downfall could hinge not on Mr. Manly's race but on the Red Shirt's hatred of a white Northerner.

"What brought you down our way?" the other Red Shirt said.

"It's a beautiful part of the country. And such friendly people. It's also excellent for my rheumatism."

The two militia men puffed up at the flattery, but just as I began to believe they would let us go, the first Red Shirt wrinkled his nose and said to his companion, "Do you smell something funny? Like . . ." He thought for a moment. "Like a privy?"

I was surprised he could smell anything over the stench of alcohol. Then I remembered the tunnel—the reeking tunnel.

To my surprise, I heard myself saying, "It ain't the smell of stinkpots, is it? 'Cause I been emptying 'em out good all day."

I had never before made myself sound uneducated, not even when I worked in the okra fields, and I was glad Daddy wasn't there to hear me. But the answer seemed to satisfy the Red Shirts, and they waved us through.

Once we reached the sawmill and I showed them the back way, there were no more Red Shirts.

We arrived at the train station north of town with

only five minutes to spare and were just able to get Mr. Manly on the train. He thanked us and asked Mr. Hanson to tell his wife that he was safe and would contact her as soon as he could. Then he turned to me and said, "Moses, tell your daddy that I'm leaving the paper in his capable hands." I took his extended hand, but I was too worn out to give him the kind of firm shake that would have made Daddy proud.

It was after supper when I got home, and I was tired and hungry. Boo Nanny and Mama hugged me and made a fuss over me, hovering like two mother hens. "Honey, we been fretting ourselves silly," Mama said.

"I'm gone fix you up some supper," Boo Nanny said.

"Where have you been?" Daddy said. "Your mother and grandmother have been out of their heads with worry. I've been out walking the streets."

"I helped Mr. Manly escape," I said, smiling broadly.

"You *what?*" His voice cracked, and a look of confusion came over him.

I thought he would be impressed by my bravery, so I was taken aback when, after I recounted my adventure, he erupted, "Have you taken leave of your senses? What were you thinking?"

I'd expected to be treated as a hero, and here he was dressing me down.

"But what . . . what . . . I thought . . . I wanted to help. . . ." I was dangerously close to blubbering.

"That's the stupidest idea I ever heard of. What was going on in there?" he said, tapping his temple with his index finger.

More than being a coward, the thing I feared above all else was being stupid. In that, I was my father's son.

"Go to the parlor. We need to talk."

I didn't want to leave Mama and Boo Nanny, but I followed his instructions. He sat in a chair facing me.

"Do you know what a lynching is?" he said.

"Of course," I said, trying to save face. I remembered being at the dinner table several months before when he said something about a mob developing a mind of its own and punishing men for crimes they didn't commit. But what did that have to do with Mr. Manly? He clearly did the thing he was accused of—writing the editorial that got white men so stirred up. That afternoon, I had been scared of getting caught by the Red Shirts, but I hadn't considered what might have happened after that.

"You were not using your head." He glared at me, trembling with rage.

I stared right back, not quite ready to take him on, but not ready to back off, either. I had made my stand, and I couldn't let on that I didn't know what lynching was, for then he would know I'd been lying. Humiliated at my ignorance, I was also furious at him. If lynching was so important, why hadn't he told me about it? He could have given me a book on it. He could have sat me down and explained the whole thing. But lynching, like sex, fell into the category of things adults stopped talking about when children entered the room.

In an act of insolence I knew I would regret, I said, "I don't care what you think. Mr. Manly needed help, and I helped him."

"How dare you talk back to me like that!" Daddy lunged at me, and for a minute I thought he was going to hit me. But he stopped himself and slumped back in the chair and lowered his head in his hands. "I need to calm down. Now leave me be."

I went to my room, and he stomped off to the back-yard. Through the closed window, I could hear the whack of an ax and the crack of splitting wood. He didn't like to do physical work and he hated this chore above all others, so I knew how upset he must be.

Before long, Mama came in and said, "Go see your daddy by the woodpile."

"Do I have to?"

"Yes, baby, you do."

I trudged slowly, one foot in front of the other, to the far end of the yard, not knowing whether to expect a whipping or a lecture. Daddy continued working while I stood silently by the hickory stump. Pieces of split wood lay scattered about on the sand. After a few more passes with the ax, he set the tool aside, brushed off the stump, and sat down, catching his breath.

"I owe you an apology," he said. He wiped sweat and bits of wood from his face, leaving traces at his temple.

I waited for him to continue.

"When you told me what you had done, I immediately thought of all the things that could have happened. You could have gotten caught up in a lynch mob. The Red Shirts might have detained you. There could have been a chase, and an accident with the carriage. Suddenly it came to me: I might have lost you. And that undid me."

"But nothing happened. I'm fine. Here I am."

"Yes, I know. But in that moment, I realized I had failed you."

"Failed how?" He was acting peculiar, and that bothered me.

"There's a lot more ugliness out there than I've led you to believe, and I haven't prepared you for it. I saw this clearly when you told me about Mr. Manly's escape. You didn't realize the danger you were in, and because of that, I could very well have lost you. And I would have had no one to blame but myself. I've been naive. I've taught you to live in a world I wanted to exist, not one that actually does."

I didn't like all this talk about failure and mistakes. I wanted the old Daddy back, the one who was wise and sure of himself and knew what to do. Always.

"I raised you in the belief that what it took to succeed in life was the same thing that it took to be a good man: honesty and hard work, courage and curiosity, loyalty and patriotism. But we're up against something I don't understand and don't know how to adapt to. I've sheltered you from it, and in the process have made you more vulnerable."

"What's that?"

"The intractability of hate," he said.

Challenge word. I gave him a cockeyed look, and he explained: "It means something that's hard to control or cure. That certainly applies to hate, I'm finding out."

At last we were on familiar ground: words and their definitions.

He was back, the Daddy I knew, the one who would do anything in the world for me. I was tired of all this adult talk and saw an opening.

"Can I get a dog?" I said.

TEN

The night before the election, I had trouble getting to sleep, wondering what the next day would bring. I got up in the dark and crouched at my window, but the magnolia tree in our side yard blocked everything but the flames that shot up from the barrel of burning pitch at the corner. The sounds of yelling and off-key singing and the stinky smell of tar kept me up long after I returned to bed, but sometime in the night, I fell asleep.

Election day dawned, a perfect autumn morning, with gulls crying in the clear blue sky. The streets felt lazy, like a Sunday, with few people about, except for the militias.

I was instructed to stay home from school, and this time I did not protest. I had already tested the patience of my family too much with Mr. Manly's escape. Besides, I was scared.

If Daddy was scared, he didn't let on. He was out of the house early to vote before going to the *Record*.

Boo Nanny and I huddled inside all day. It was the waiting that was the worst. We waited as Mama walked to work. We waited while Daddy was out and about covering the elections. We waited for a knock on the door that would bring bad news.

Boo Nanny simmered a concoction of dried roots and herbs on the stove—to calm nerves, she said, but it only agitated me. The steam fogged the windows and filled the room with the most stomach-wrenching smell. There was no way to escape the odor, since I was confined to the kitchen. Our house sat on a corner lot, and the rooms that faced Fifth and Bladen Streets were susceptible to stray gunfire. It was a miserable day, and I couldn't wait for it to end.

That night Daddy got back late, after putting the *Record* to bed. We crowded around, eager to hear what had happened. He sat down, took off his glasses, and rubbed the bridge of his nose. His eyes were bloodshot.

"There was no violence. The voting went on without incident. The Democrats won a resounding victory, but they won it fair and square."

"You thinks our folk gone walk past these armed paddy rollers to vote? That's what you call fair?" Boo Nanny said.

"Next time, we'll just have to work harder," he sighed. But he was not yet ready to abandon his optimism. "At any rate, the Republicans still control the mayor, the chief of police, and the aldermen. We aren't up for reelection until next spring."

The morning after the election, the streets were quiet. Daddy decided that I could go to school, but he insisted on walking with me to make sure I was safe. His work and my school were in the same direction.

We reached the corner of Seventh and Market, where Daddy normally peeled off to go to his office, but he continued down Market. "I'll walk with you all the way," Daddy said.

"You don't need to do that," I said, alarmed. I didn't want my classmates to think I was like the first graders whose parents brought them to school.

"I can use the exercise."

Because we were early, no one was on the playground when we arrived. I quickly bid Daddy good-bye and scampered through the front door before anyone could see us.

At school, things were back to normal, and no one talked about the election. After class, I came straight home and was surprised to find Daddy in the kitchen, reading the *Messenger*. The headline read: "Negroism Defunct."

"What are you doing here?" I asked. It was so strange to find Daddy home at this hour.

"A businessman named Mr. Williams asked to see me. He didn't want to come by my place of work, so I agreed to meet him here."

When a knock came at the door, I answered it. Mr. Williams was a slight, middle-aged man with eyebrows so light, it looked as if he had no eyebrows at all. He stood at the door with his hat in his hand. I introduced myself and shook his hand. He was definitely not a person of character, I decided, because he had a limp handshake and refused to look me in the eye.

I invited him inside, but he wanted to stay on the porch, even though it was chilly.

"Please come into the parlor," I said, knowing that Mama would be mortified at the condition of the front porch. Leaves had collected there, as if it were an abandoned house, since Boo Nanny and Mama had avoided being outside for the two weeks leading up to the election.

Daddy came out to the porch and shook Mr. Williams's hand. "What can I help you with?" Daddy said.

Mr. Williams glanced around, as if expecting someone to pop out from behind a door or spring from behind a chair.

I sat down and felt leaves crush against my backside. Daddy didn't ask me to leave as I thought he would.

Mr. Williams took a seat on the edge of the rocker, causing it to tilt forward. He put his hat on his knees and cleared his throat. "A group of concerned citizens, the Committee of Twenty-Five, has been appalled by the growing violence that has overtaken our city. We feel that something must be done about it."

"I couldn't agree more," Daddy said. "You look uncomfortable. Wouldn't you prefer the swing?"

"No, I'm fine here," he said, and looked as if he'd lost his place, like someone interrupted in the middle of a memorized poem who must return to the beginning to be able to recite it all the way through.

"Now, I know you love our great city and want to do what is best," he continued.

Daddy nodded and kept looking at him as the man shifted his weight, causing the floor to creak.

"Well, I—that is to say, the Committee of Twenty-Five—felt that, in light of the threat of violence . . ."

"These concerned citizens—this Committee of Twenty-Five, as you say—who might they be?"

Mr. Williams rattled off a list of names.

"This afternoon, I received notice that I was to attend a meeting at six-thirty tonight at the Cape Fear Club. Is this organized by the same group?"

He nodded.

"So these concerned citizens you named—I believe

they're all white, am I right? What exactly is it that they're concerned about?"

"We must do something to calm the city. It is our responsibility as community leaders."

"And who elected this so-called committee? Were their names on the ballot yesterday?"

"No. They're civic leaders. The backbone of the community. The men who make things work. They were chosen by a group of citizens who gathered at the county courthouse this morning."

"I see," Daddy said. "And were there any Negroes in this group?"

Mr. Williams ignored the question and continued. "I appeal to your good citizenship. You are an articulate spokesman, a pillar of the colored community. I know you'll be willing to do the right thing. That's why I volunteered to come talk with you. If you care about our Port City, then you'll agree with me that we need to start with a new government, a clean slate."

"I believe yesterday's election achieved that."

"But that was for state and county offices. We need a fresh start with a new slate for city government."

"And how might that be achieved?"

"With your cooperation."

Daddy stared at Mr. Williams in disbelief. "Wait a minute. Are you asking me to resign as alderman?" he said.

"Believe me when I say prejudice has nothing to do with this. It is not a question of color. We've also requested the mayor, the chief of police, and the . . ."

"And anyone who is favorable to our race," Daddy said. "In other words, you're asking all the democratically elected city representatives to voluntarily give up their jobs because a self-appointed group of white Democrats determined that it is best for the city?"

"It's for the good of your people as well."

Daddy stood up. "I'll ask you nicely to please leave now." When he was about to explode, Daddy kept control of his voice but could be really, really scary. I know. I almost felt sorry for Mr. Williams.

The white man shifted in his seat. "Now don't get upset. All I'm asking is that you consider what's best for Wilmington. We must do something to restore peace and harmony. It's bad for business. It's bad for the reputation of our city."

"Maybe you should have thought of that before you launched this despicable white supremacy campaign. You can't preach hate and then shirk responsibility for the way hate is manifested."

"My, you seem angry."

"Angry? I'd say that's a fair appraisal. The Democrats won the state and county elections at the ballot box, fair and square, though I'm beginning to question how fair the elections actually were. But what you're proposing, what you're asking me to do, is completely different. You're asking me to participate in a coup d'état," Daddy said.

Challenge word. I would have to look that one up later.

Mr. Williams seemed startled. "I wouldn't call it that. Now, if your people hadn't threatened violence . . ."

"My people, as you call us, had no weapons, no organization. We were helpless against a city in which heavily armed militias, private vigilance committees, and self-appointed Red Shirts ruled the neighborhood. We didn't have a chance."

A sneeze tickled my nose. I didn't want to call attention to myself and tried to stop it, but it came on anyway.

Mr. Williams looked in my direction, seemed to be confused for a moment, but then continued. "We feel that your people would be better off if calm was restored to the Port City. You have to think of their welfare. They will benefit from safe streets."

Daddy still didn't raise his voice and continued to be courteous, but his words were fueled by conviction. "Let me tell you something. My wife was born into slavery, but grew up to know what freedom and opportunity are like. And my wife's mother, she's working out in the backyard right now. She lived her first thirty years as a slave, bought and sold like the mules that you trade at market. For the past week, these two women have been cowering inside the house in fear."

"My point exactly," Mr. Williams said.

"Hear me out."

Mr. Williams looked around, as if for an escape route.

"And my son sitting here beside you, he's a smart boy. He wants to go to college. He will do great things in the world. We live in Wilmington because it's a good place to raise a family. There's opportunity. He has role models with people of color in the police and fire departments, as aldermen."

"We're not asking you to leave the city," Mr. Williams said.

"Please, let me finish. That boy, I'm so proud of him, and I want him to be proud of me. How's he going to do that if I cave in to the ridiculous demands of a mob that has stolen the elections, ignited violence, and then pointed fingers at the most powerless people on the political ladder?" He walked to the head of the steps. "No, Mr. Williams, I will not resign as alderman. I was democratically elected. You go back and tell that self-appointed Committee of Twenty-Five that if the people in my ward want me out, there's a way for them to express their wishes. It's called an election, and by my calendar, it's not scheduled until next spring."

"Well, I'm . . . I must say . . . I'm quite surprised. You are quite . . . quite distressed. I thought you'd be capable of reason."

"Now get off my porch, before I do something that will justify your view of my race."

Mr. Williams scurried down the steps. In his flight, he reached up to his bare head and realized he had left his hat behind, but made no effort to return to get it.

I watched Daddy standing at the top of the steps, twirling the man's hat on his finger. I had never been so proud of him.

Daddy invited me to go to the 6:30 meeting of the Committee of Twenty-Five at the Cape Fear Club. "It's an important part of your education," he said.

I felt grown-up, having Daddy include me. If the other twenty-four members of the committee were anything like Mr. Williams, it would be an interesting meeting indeed.

We zigzagged our way to the Cape Fear Club, avoiding the streets patrolled by Red Shirts. The election had passed peacefully, but the militias remained on the streets and people in Darktown stayed indoors.

I was familiar with the Cape Fear Club—everyone in Wilmington was. The brick mansion near the waterfront had four white columns and verandas across the first and second floors. This was where the blue bloods of Wilmington gathered to eat, play cards, and socialize. The only Negroes allowed inside were butlers, maids, and janitors. Mama earned extra money cleaning up after the annual masquerade ball, when Wilmington society turned out in feathered and sequined masks and fancy costumes. Even among white people, it was hard to get an invitation.

Daddy and I approached the mansion by the side door. Other prominent citizens from the Negro community walked up silently with long faces, as if at a funeral. I recognized Lewis's father, along with the owner of a pawnshop, our family doctor, and a lawyer friend of Daddy's.

At the side door, a bearded white man in formal dress stopped us while he looked for Daddy's name on the list.

"The boy will have to leave. No children allowed," the man said gruffly.

"He's my son. He'll sit quietly and won't be any trouble," Daddy assured him.

"None of your kind enters here without permission."

"Could he wait for me in the back hall until we're done?"

"Most certainly not."

"But it's dangerous on the streets," Daddy said.

"Your choice," the man said. "Now step aside."

Daddy looked uncomfortable. Other Negroes filed in and were checked off the list. Finally Daddy put a hand on my shoulder and said, "Wait for us at David Jacobs's barbershop. You know the one on Dock Street, right? You'll be safe there, and it's only a few blocks away. Will you be all right? Are you scared?"

I shook my head no, but it was a lie. I only felt brave when Daddy was around. But the barbershop wasn't far, so I ran all the way there as fast as I could and arrived out of breath.

After only twenty minutes, Negroes from the meeting started arriving at the barbershop. Before long, some thirty men had squeezed into the small space with three barber chairs. The large mirrors on facing walls made it look as if twice as many people were there. The men were as noisy here as they had been silent filing into the Cape Fear Club. Daddy was one of the last to arrive. He searched the crowd, and when he found me, he nodded and smiled.

Everyone was speaking at once. I picked up the words *document, Declaration of Independence,* and *deadline.* From what I could gather, the white men had presented the colored citizens with an ultimatum and demanded a response by 7:30 the following morning.

Dr. Hudson, our family doctor, stood nearby with a

document in his hand. I asked if I could take a look. He handed it to me.

Angling the paper so the lantern lit the surface, I began to read. Across the top, in spidery penmanship, were the words "White Declaration of Independence."

Believing that the Constitution of the United States contemplated a government to be carried on by an enlightened people; Believing that its framers did not anticipate the enfranchisement of an ignorant population of African origin, and believing that those men of the State of North Carolina, who joined in forming the Union, did not contemplate for their descendants subjection to an inferior race:

We, the undersigned citizens of the City of Wilmington and County of New Hanover, do hereby declare that we will no longer be ruled, and will never again be ruled by men of African origin.

Before I could get any further, Daddy stood on a table and called for everyone to be quiet. I handed the document back to Dr. Hudson.

Daddy opened a discussion about how to proceed.

"Why don't we respond point by point?" someone said. "How many points are there?"

"Seven," came the response from the back of the room.

Lewis's father asked Daddy to read the first and fourth points.

"Who has the copy?" Daddy said, and Dr. Hudson handed him the document. Daddy's voice was clear and strong as he read: "'First: That the time has passed for the intelligent citizens of the community owning ninety percent of the property and paying taxes in like proportion, to be ruled by Negroes.'

"And the fourth point is as follows," he said. "'That the progressive element in any community is the white population and that the giving of nearly all the employment to Negro laborers has been against the best interests of this County and City and is sufficient reason why the City of Wilmington, with its natural advantages, has not become a city of at least fifty thousand inhabitants.'"

Lewis's father, owner of a bank and lots of rental property, spoke up: "So, do I have this right? On the one hand, they're saying that us no-count, shiftless colored folk don't have jobs and don't pay taxes. Then in the very next breath, they say the coloreds are taking jobs away from the whites and must be stopped. That doesn't make any sense. Which way is it?"

A roar of anger swelled up from the crowd. Light from the lanterns bounced from one mirror to another, giving the room the impression of being ablaze.

"It doesn't matter. We can't react to this logically," Daddy said. "There is no logic."

Mr. Walker, the grocer, was the next to speak. "If we can't get things quieted down, I can't make a profit. With folks terrified to venture out these past two weeks, I gots fruit rotting on my shelves. I say give whitey what he wants and get our people back on the streets, spending money."

A murmur passed through the crowd. In the mirror, I could see Daddy from the front and back.

Upon request, he summarized the fifth point, which said that in the future, all jobs would go to white men. The last two points demanded that the *Record* cease publication, and that Alexander Manly leave Wilmington or the citizens would take him by force.

I waited for Daddy to announce that Mr. Manly had already left town, but on this point he was silent.

A man near me said, "We don't have nothing to do with Mr. Manly's editorial. He doesn't speak for us all."

"Exactly. Good point. That's what we put in the response," offered Mr. Bainbridge, who owned a funeral home.

"What do they want from us?" came a shout from the crowd.

"That we say 'yes, massa,' 'no, massa,' then shuck and jive back to the plantation." It was Salem Bell speaking. He owned a fish and oyster business at the Front Street Market.

"Why didn't you speak up at the Cape Fear Club, when it counted? I saw you slinking out of there, hat in hand."

"Quiet, Charles," Daddy said. "You were at the meeting. You know they didn't allow any questions or discussion of any kind."

Everyone broke out speaking at once and the room was filled with chatter until Daddy got everyone quieted down.

"We'll never get anywhere if we try to answer point by point. We have to step back and look at the bigger picture."

From the crowd came a murmur of approval.

"The white citizens have presented us with a cowardly document—saying they know best, writing their own Declaration of Independence, as if the original document needed improving."

Daddy paused a moment. The room was so quiet you could hear the lantern flames flutter.

"It is now thirty-five years since Emancipation. No one appreciates the right to vote more than those who have been denied it for so long. Anything is possible as long as we have the vote. We cannot let them take away that power without a fight."

Daddy's shadow lurched and swayed overhead like a black ghost.

"They want us to give up our manhood, our self-respect, and our faith in the future. And they want us to do it voluntarily. Well, my friends, do I have any volunteers?"

"Nooooo!" bellowed the men in the room, drawing the word out into a lowing sound, like a barn full of cows.

"I have been asked to resign as alderman, along with any white men who support Negro rights, including the mayor and the chief of police."

"That's not legal," said David Jacobs. He owned the barbershop and also served as Negro coroner.

"Exactly, and this kind of illegal action calls for a firm response. But we must proceed carefully, respectfully. It's a delicate balance. There can be no violence, no actions that can be used to reproach us."

A man I didn't recognize turned to me. "Your daddy's going to get us out of this. He's the only leader we have," he said, and patted me on the shoulder.

"There is not one Constitution for white folks and a separate one for black folks. There is one Constitution for all Americans, no matter what the color of their skin, and it promises us the right to vote. This is what we are guaranteed, and we will settle for nothing less."

I recognized a little of the old Daddy—cautious, measured, polite. But in other ways, he was totally changed. He was moving the men to action with his words.

"We will not roll over and let them rewrite the Constitution without a fight. And we *will* fight—not for ourselves, but for our children. That's what's at stake, and it is everything." He looked toward my corner and nodded.

"I aspire to a world in which my son can become whatever his talents and his vision combine to make him. A world where, if he works hard and treats others with respect, there is no limit to what he can accomplish. As a parent and as a citizen, this is what matters most to me."

Sounds of approval broke out among the crowd.

"In yesterday's election for state and county offices, the Democrats caught us off guard. They used Negro baiting, hatred, and fear to win at the ballot box. And win they did. We need to acknowledge that. What we cannot allow them to do is consolidate those gains by doing what no city in the history of America has ever done: overthrow the legally elected city government."

From the crowd came cries of "Amen" and "Tell it, brother," like at a church revival. Daddy seemed to feed off the energy of the crowd.

"But we will not surrender. Right is on our side. The Constitution is on our side. We will prevail!"

Cheers erupted. Someone threw his hat into the air.

Others followed. Fists were raised. I knew I was witnessing something extraordinary. I decided then and there that I didn't want to be a fireman; I wanted to be a political leader.

The men in the barbershop appointed the lawyer Armond Scott to deliver the group's response to Alfred Waddell's house by 7:30 the following morning. When the meeting turned to the more boring job of drafting a response to the White Declaration of Independence, I sat in one of the barber chairs and waited for Daddy.

When we arrived home, two plates of food were waiting in the kitchen. I told Boo Nanny and Mama about the evening in as much detail as I could recall. They exchanged worried glances.

"Lord, what's the world coming to?" Mama said.

"You should have seen Daddy. He was unbelievable. He had everyone's attention." I was mad that they didn't understand how important the meeting was, and what a major part Daddy had played.

"Trouble be a-brewing. I can feel it," Boo Nanny moaned, washing her hands with invisible soap.

"How?" The older I got, the less I trusted her superstitions.

"Like the rain that whispers to my bones afore it comes," she said.

Around nine, someone knocked at the front door. I

heard low voices, then Daddy said loudly, "What do you mean? How can this be?"

After more hushed talking, I heard Daddy say, "No, it's completely understandable. I'll see what I can do."

When he came back to the kitchen, he told me what had happened. On the way to deliver the group's response to Alfred Waddell, Armond Scott had run into a group of drunk and rowdy Red Shirts, who bunched around him and shoved him against a tree. He got scared, and instead of continuing through the white neighborhood to deliver the message, he dropped it in the mailbox. Mr. Waddell would receive the response the following day, but not by the 7:30 a.m. deadline.

"What happens if he doesn't get it?" I asked.

"I don't know," Daddy said. "I'll stop by his house tomorrow and let him know what happened."

ELEVEN

Boo Nanny shaded her eyes and looked up at the sky. "Keep an eye out. I don't likes what I sees," she said.

It was the following morning, and I was in the back-yard doing my daily chores before school. The air was heavy and felt like rain. Gulls and buzzards flew overhead—white specks and black specks that kept to separate parts of the sky.

"Trouble's a-brewing," she said, watching the buzzards.

I no longer believed in omens. No buzzards dotted the sky on election day, or the day after, and trouble was brewing then, for sure.

On my way back from the woodpile, Boo Nanny said, "Git your body inside, quick." She pushed me so hard toward the porch that I stumbled and dropped an arm-load of wood. My chin hit the top step just as a buzzard swooped down low toward the house.

"His shadow didn't get me," I assured her so she wouldn't worry. I put my fingers to my chin to see if I was bleeding. I was.

"Don't matter. Old Mr. Buzzard, he back. Today be a bad-news day."

"How do you know?" I said, gathering the wood I had dropped and putting it by the back door.

"That ol' buzzard set hisself down on our chimbley like he owned the place. Trouble be on the way, for true." Boo Nanny hugged me tight. "You is the sweetest thing that ever lived or died, and I loves you to pieces, Cocoa Baby."

I wriggled out from her grip. She looked hurt, but I was too old to believe in omens and too old to be hugged like a little baby.

Before I left for school, she dabbed the cut on my chin with a salve. Maybe my classmates would think I nicked myself shaving.

Daddy came onto the porch and said, "Are you ready?"

I tightened my book strap and started to leave, but Boo Nanny stopped me. "Your coat. You'll catch your death," she said. She went inside and returned with my corduroy jacket.

To humor her, I put it on, and Daddy and I started off together. It was two days after the election, and he still insisted on walking me to school. But first, he told me, he needed to go by Mr. Waddell's house to let him know that the Negro community's response to the ultimatum would be delayed by several hours. Mr. Waddell lived on Fifth Street, just like us, but across the bridge and closer to Market, where the rich people lived.

We stopped at an enormous clapboard and shingle house that had a round tower, like a lighthouse, with a conical hat on top. We went to the front door and Daddy knocked.

A middle-aged lady answered. Daddy took off his hat and held it in front of him.

"Good morning, ma'am. I'm here to see Alfred Waddell," he said with his usual flawless manners.

"Go around to the back and someone will receive you."

"I will not," he said firmly but politely. "My name is Jack Thomas. I have a matter of the utmost urgency to discuss with Mr. Waddell. Would you be so kind as to give him the message?"

She closed the door and locked it, then retreated. Through the glass window in the front door, I looked into a small room between the porch and hallway—a kind of intermediate porch. On the floor was an elaborate mosaic in a star pattern. Beyond that, I could see through the leaded glass of the second front door into a wood-paneled hall. The walls looked like shadow-box frames set side by side, row upon row, but in the middle, where the picture would normally be, was plain dark wood. The house was fancier than the Gilchrists', where Mama worked.

While we waited on the porch, I reached into my pocket and felt something foreign. I slipped it out and saw that it was a pouch made from flour sacking and puffed out with dried herbs, a nest of hair, and small twigs, or maybe even bones. I quickly returned it to my pocket and smiled. Boo Nanny had sent along protection. It was our secret.

Before long, a bearded man in a bright red corduroy vest came out on the porch and closed the door behind him. I felt my heart go icy. I recognized the man. It was Daddy's nemesis, the man who had stood on the steps of Thalian Hall and said that the Cape Fear River would be choked with black carcasses. The man's cold gray eyes stared at us.

"What do you mean, Jack, terrifying my wife? What do you have to say for yourself?"

"I'm sorry, Alfred. That was not my intention."

The white man's white beard trembled with anger at something Daddy said, but I didn't know what. Daddy continued: "I had to get an important message to you this morning. The lawyer we entrusted with delivering the response from the Negro citizens was met by an angry mob. He became frightened and posted our response instead of bringing it to your door. You will not receive the document by the seven-thirty deadline."

"That is most unfortunate." He scowled. "We had a deadline for a reason."

"Yes, but you'll agree the circumstances were unavoidable. The document should be at your house with the morning mail. Will you please alert all parties that need to be informed?"

He nodded, but did not look happy.

"You should also know that Alexander Manly left town several days ago, under threat of violence. He is no longer in the city," Daddy said.

"Preposterous," Mr. Waddell said. "The railroads, wharf, and roads were all surrounded by guards."

"Be that as it may, he is gone, I assure you."

"Then Wilmington has rid itself of the vilest slanderer in North Carolina."

I squeezed the pouch of herbs in my pocket to steady my trembling hand.

"I beg you most respectfully to convey to your men that the Negro community is in no way responsible for, nor do we in any way condone, the editorial Mr. Manly wrote."

"It's a little late for that," he said.

"People are riled up. Fears and emotions are high. The pot needs no more fuel to set it boiling," Daddy said.

"Are you telling me what to do?" Mr. Waddell said.

"No, I'm only stating what we both know to be true. Good day," he said.

I was relieved when Mr. Waddell went back inside and we put some distance between us.

"Daddy, why did that man get so worked up when you said you were sorry?"

"I called him by his first name. He thought I was acting above my station."

We walked in silence and turned left on Market Street, where the houses got smaller and smaller the farther away from the river you went. At Seventh Street, where Daddy usually turned off to go to his work, I tried to convince him to let me go the rest of the way by myself. We compromised, and he walked with me a few blocks farther east on Market but let me turn and go the last block by myself.

Midmorning, I was playing shinny outside at first recess when I heard crowd noises like a baseball game coming over the trees, in the direction of downtown. Curious, I dropped my stick and slipped away from the playground.

A slight rise in Market Street prevented me from

seeing anything, but a great racket of cheering, whistles, and shouts filled the air. I walked toward the river, and soon, several blocks down, I saw a mass of white men walking toward me. A parade, I thought, but as I got to the corner of Eighth Street I saw that many were carrying guns and swords. The men in the front marched in military fashion, eight abreast. Farther back, the organization fell apart, and the men crowded randomly in the street. As they proceeded down Market, men streamed from off porches and side streets to join them.

Mr. Waddell was in the lead, carrying a Winchester rifle. I recognized him by his red vest. Instantly I knew that this was not a parade. Angry shouts rose from the crowd: "String up Manly!" "Rid the city of the pest!"

With horror, I realized they were headed for the *Record*.

I ducked behind a camellia bush and watched to see if the white mob would turn onto Seventh and march into the black neighborhood, where the narrow shotgun houses with tin roofs were built close together. Sure enough, the procession rounded the corner, with Mr. Waddell in the lead. At the sight of the marchers, Negro women screamed and herded their little ones inside.

I knew I had to reach Daddy before the mob did. Sprinting through the backyards of the houses that faced Seventh Street, I leaped over fences, dodged out-houses and wells, scattered chickens, and set dogs to barking.

Once I got to Love and Charity Hall, I dashed up the stairs to the *Record* offices. Daddy was at his desk editing copy. Gasping for air, I tried to tell him what I'd seen.

"Slow down. Catch your breath," he said.

"There's no time. A mob's coming. Hundreds and hundreds of them, and they all have guns. That Waddell man is in the lead. They're coming down Seventh. Quick. Look out the window. They'll be here any minute."

By this time, some of the staff had gathered around. I was hot and sweaty from running, and hung my jacket on the coatrack.

"There's reason to be alarmed, but not alarmist," Daddy said calmly. "Let me go check."

I followed him and several members of the staff to the window, and we looked down the street. Far from exaggerating, I had underestimated the crowd. It trailed back for blocks.

When the front line reached the *Record*, Mr. Waddell raised his Winchester and called for the men to stop.

"Get back," Daddy said, herding the half dozen men to the center of the room.

Through the window we heard shouts: "Fumigate the city with the *Record*!" "Lynch Manly!" "Hand him over! We'll give him justice he deserves!" There were also cries of "Save our womanhood!" and "Give up the nigger!"

Men raised their guns angrily, but no one fired.

Daddy remained calm, and that helped soothe the frayed nerves of the other men—the office manager, a pressman, a few typesetters, and a reporter.

"They've come for our editor," Daddy said.

"But he's left town," the reporter said.

"The crowd doesn't know that," Daddy said.

"But you told Mr. Waddell this morning," I said.

"Evidently he did not relay that information to the mob."

"Go out and tell them he's gone," the reporter said. "Reason with them."

"You's crazy in de head. They out for blood. They gone kill us poor folk," the typesetter said, shaking.

"I've devoted my life to reason and it's done no good," Daddy said. "You can't reason across the table from hatred."

There was a banging at the double doors that led to the outside staircase.

"What we gone do?" one of the typesetters said. His eyes widened in an unmistakable display of terror.

The battering and shouts at the door continued. Daddy spoke in an urgent but steady voice. "James, I'm putting you in charge of getting everyone to the supply room," he said to the pressman. "Keep Moses with you. I'm going to help the ladies downstairs. They must be in a state. We'll get through this. Now go! Time is of the essence."

He went down the interior stairs, and the pressman herded the employees into the back supply room, where the newsprint was stored. I was last in line. Before I could leave, the front door splintered and the mob surged in. I crawled under a desk and wrapped myself into a small package with my arms around my knees. I could feel my heart thumping rapidly against my thighs. In the room, there were angry shouts. Desks were overturned. Glass crashed.

I was afraid that my hiding place would be toppled over like the others, so I crawled on all fours to the coatrack. Peeking from behind the jackets, I saw a man put on Mr. Manly's beaver hat and do a loose-jointed dance. Framed photographs were heaved out through the window. A typewriter followed.

A dozen men gathered around the printing press and, groaning under the weight, carried the big, burly black brute out the double doors, maneuvered it onto the banister, and tipped it over. Cheers erupted from the crowd outside as the press crashed to the ground.

A man took the butt of his shotgun and smashed the

lanterns hanging on the wall. Clear liquid dripped down and pooled on the floor.

Another man sprinkled a large can of kerosene over the papers that littered the floor.

"Who's got a match?" he said. I burrowed farther into the coats.

"Stop. We've done what we've come to do. Let's get out of here," one man said.

"Someone's got to finish this off."

"Out! Quick! This place is gonna blow!"

Footsteps thundered toward the door, then silence. After a while, I heard the faintest crackle at the other end of the room, like the kindling tepee that started off Boo Nanny's morning fire under the laundry kettle. I stayed behind the coats until I was sure that all the white men had gone. When I emerged from my hiding place, a cold salt breeze came through the broken glass and lifted the small tongues of orange in the corner, causing them to grow. In a flash, flames zipped along the line of spilled kerosene and nipped at the newspapers that were scattered everywhere.

Fire climbed the wall with amazing speed and lapped at the rafters, following the wet kerosene tracks on the wall. Soon the fire reached the ceiling. Then the far end of the building burst into flames.

Paralyzed with fear, I watched the flames consume

the paper and wood. When movement came back to my limbs, I started toward the supply room in the back. At that moment, I heard a sound like the crack of thunder, and a rafter engulfed in orange crashed down on the coatrack, narrowly missing me. Now I was surrounded by shooting fountains of fire.

Trapped, I searched for other exits. The front door, in full flame, was out of the question. The other way was blocked by the fallen roof. The room filled rapidly with smoke. My eyes teared up, and I started coughing. I was feeling light-headed and disoriented. Around me the flapping flames sounded like clothes on a line in a heavy wind. Through the smoke, someone called my name.

It was Daddy. He had come back for me but couldn't see me. I tried to answer, but like the dream I sometimes had, I opened my mouth and nothing came out. Fear had robbed my vocal cords of their abilities.

I saw a typewriter on the desk. In desperation, I returned the carriage by way of the silver lever and a small ding came out. I began some wild two-fingered typing, returning the carriage over and over, hoping the sound would signal my whereabouts. I felt my legs buckle, and before I hit the ground, I was out.

When I came to, I found my cheek against Daddy's back. He had slung me over his shoulder like a sack of yams. He carried me outside and placed me on the lawn between Love and Charity Hall and St. Luke's Baptist Church. He held a tin cup of water to my lips.

His eyes were wet, and at first I thought the smoke had gotten to him. But his shoulders shook and he hugged me tight, and I started crying, too, more scared than ever now that the danger had passed.

"I thought you were gone. I thought I'd lost you," he said.

Soon he regained his composure and took a sip of water himself.

The second floor of the building was now in full flame. Fist-sized chunks of soot floated in the air like so many crows. Glowing sprays of embers shot toward the church. Ashes, like moths, flew skyward.

Some white men were on the roofs of the surrounding houses, beating at the fire with jackets and blankets. Most milled about in the street, watching the building burn.

The printing press lay on its head, burrowed into the sand, mangled and misshapen like a wrecked locomotive. All the things that couldn't burn—typewriters, the printing press—had been tossed outside. The things that could burn—wooden desks, newsprint—were inside, feeding the hungry plumes of red, yellow, and orange that competed with each other over which could reach highest into the sky.

"Where are the fire trucks? The alarm sounded a while ago." The voice belonged to one of the Negroes who huddled together near the steps of the church, amid the larger crowd of armed white men.

"They's stopped at Sixth and Castle. I seed 'em. Those horses champing at the bit and the boys doing all they can to hold them back."

"That doesn't sound right. I know those boys. That's the finest Negro fire unit in the city," Daddy said.

"Old Tuck Savage was sent by the fire chief to hold 'em back. That's what I heared. They wants to make good and sure this place burns to the ground afore letting 'em through."

Daddy stood up, furious. "I'll see about that."

"What you gots a mind to do?"

"I don't care if those firemen are black or white. They're professionals. The only color they hate is red. It goes against the grain for them to stand by and let a fire burn."

"Careful, now, Mr. Thomas. You's all we gots."

Daddy bent down and patted me on the head. "I'll be right back," he said, and strode off.

I was shivering. The sun had gone behind the clouds, and the sky threatened rain—exactly what we needed. But like the firemen, the rain held itself back. One of the Love Ladies brought a jacket and put it around me. It was a ladies' jacket, pinched in at the waist with a little flounce below, but I was too cold to protest. What I really wanted was my jacket with Boo Nanny's protective pouch in the pocket, but it had gone up in flames with the rest of the building.

Before long, I heard a clanging bell. The crowd parted to make room for the horses that dashed madly up the street, pulling the steam engine behind. The large upright brass boiler chuffed black smoke from its stack, which mingled with the smoke in the air. The gleaming brass and nickel pumps reflected the fire in flashes and glints, like a sunset. Another pair of horses followed with the hook and ladder.

Red was a color I had come to fear and despise, but the Negro firemen in their red firefighting togs were a welcome sight indeed. As they pulled up, gunfire crackled into the air. The firemen didn't pay it any mind. Moving quickly and efficiently, they hooked the hoses to the fire hydrant and the steam engine, and the armed men did nothing to stop them. Two muscular firemen stood on either side of the hose, trying to control the weaving and jerking as a pressurized geyser of cold water shot toward the second floor, which by now was completely destroyed, with nothing but the north wall left standing. But the first floor and the surrounding buildings could be saved.

Daddy returned, and together we watched the firemen battle the flames. By the time the fire was finally under control, the white crowd had thinned out considerably. Several dozen men posed in front of the smoldering remains, holding their weapons. The front line crouched down as a photographer set up his box on stilts and disappeared under the hood. With a poof, he added his own puff of smoke to the air and documented the moment for all to remember.

Overhead, buzzards soared in the sky.

"Stop by the Gilchrists' and tell your mother to go home immediately. Then keep Boo Nanny out of the backyard. I want you all inside. Hurry. You don't have much time," Daddy said.

"But school . . ."

"Not today. There's going to be trouble."

Surely he was not referring to the buzzards. But for whatever reason, on this one point, he and Boo Nanny were in perfect agreement.

TWELVE

Colonel Gilchrist's house, where Mama worked, was on Third Street, closer to the wharf. I knocked on the back door and was surprised when a white woman answered. She had light hair and wore a Sunday dress on Thursday. Her skin was the color of a parsnip.

"Sadie, there's a poor little ragamuffin out back. See what he wants," she said.

Mama appeared behind the white woman and pulled me inside by the stove. She licked her thumb and furiously rubbed it across my cheek to get rid of the soot. "Miss Ellen, this be my boy, Moses," she murmured, and looked down, ashamed.

The white lady backed away from me as if separating herself from a bad smell.

"Baby, what happened to you?" Mama whispered.

"There was a fire at the *Record*. A mob burned it

down," I said, speaking fast. "Daddy says you need to go home right away."

"Honey, I can't," she said, glancing nervously at Mrs. Gilchrist.

"Please, Mama. You have to," I said, desperate. It was my responsibility to get her home. I had promised. "Daddy says there's going to be trouble in the streets."

"Mercy me. There's no cause for trouble," said Mrs. Purse-Lipped Parsnip. "My husband was there. He said it was a procession of perfectly sober men. No one was injured. And they succeeded in ridding the city of that appalling Negro paper."

Clearly she didn't know anything about our family. Ignoring her, I continued with Mama. "Daddy says it isn't safe. He doesn't want you on the street after dark."

Mama squeezed the hem of her apron in her fist and looked nervously at me, then at Mrs. Gilchrist. "Can I haves the afternoon off?"

"But who will fix dinner and take care of Edward when he gets up from his nap?" Mrs. Gilchrist said.

Mama looked miserable.

"Sadie, you're a good sort of Negro. You have served me faithfully, and I have no complaints about your work. But I can find another," she said.

I hated her for making Mama feel small.

"Run along, Moses. I be home the usual time," she said.

From Mama's place of work, I went down Nun to Front Street, past the Sprunt mansion, with palm trees in front and a set of massive white columns that dwarfed the ones at the Cape Fear Club. What was it with white people and columns?

Mr. Sprunt owned the largest cotton compress in town. White people called his workers Sprunt Niggers because on weekends, when the men splurged on bars and ended up in jail, Mr. Sprunt bailed them out.

I turned on Front Street and walked toward the business district. Nothing seemed out of the ordinary until a trolley clanged past and white men fired guns out the window and made a racket with shouts of "We got 'em! We burned the *Record!*" The trolley stopped, and the men emptied out and joined a crowd that had gathered in front of the YMCA.

A fire bell started to ring, and I panicked. Two fires in the same day was more than I could take. The best thing to do, I decided, was to go toward the wharf. If necessary, I could jump into the river. I ducked into the first alley I came to and cut over to the waterfront.

I found myself in front of the giant Sprunt Cotton Compress. Equipment operators, cotton processors, ticket collectors, and laborers of all kinds streamed out of the building, bewildered. Stevedores abandoned the bales they were loading and left them on the dock.

"They burned de *Record*, and now they's burning our homes. It be de devil's own work!" someone shouted.

The crowd swelled as more people spilled out of the warehouse. The fire bell kept ringing. Some Negroes pointed to the sky, looking for smoke.

I looked up Walnut Street. The white men who had congregated in front of the YMCA were now marching toward the compress. The Sprunt workers far outnumbered the whites, but the white men were armed. The workers fell back, creating chaos as some tried to exit while others tried to reenter the building. No one knew which way to turn. Afraid of getting caught in between, I crossed the street to blend in with the workers.

A black man sprinted down the alley from Front Street and into the crowd of laborers, yelling, "Oh my Lord, the Red Shirts have killed one man and they gone butcher us all!" He ran inside toward a huge mound of loose cotton and dived in, disappearing into the downy pile.

Hundreds of panicked workers began churning, not knowing which way to turn. A white foreman tried to calm them.

A tiny, weasel-headed white man climbed on top of a

pyramid of compressed cotton bales. I could tell by the way the workers stood at attention that this was Mr. Sprunt, the owner, whose house I had passed earlier. "Men, men. Quiet. I know you're worried about your families. I sent a trusted employee into the community. You all know George." He pointed to someone in the crowd of all black faces. "He tells me that other than the *Record*, there are no houses on fire. There is no violence. The rumors you're hearing are only that. Rumors."

The men murmured among themselves. I thought of what Daddy used to say: "Fear turns men's brains to mush."

Mr. Sprunt continued: "The bells are calling out the militia. I urge calm. If you want to go home, I'll have someone escort you through the sentries, but I beg you, go back to your stations."

"What have we done? We have no weapons," came a voice from among the black faces.

Mr. Sprunt turned to the angry white men who had amassed on the other side of the street. "My men are unarmed. You, all of you, disperse, I beg of you."

His plea had little effect on the throng, which bubbled and frothed like boiling navy beans. Someone in the white crowd hollered, "Let's kill the whole gang of 'em!"

From his platform, the little man with the big house shouted, "Shoot if you will, but make me the victim!"

This seemed to confuse the white men.

Mr. Sprunt's voice boomed: "All my workers, back inside. I'm barricading the door. We'll protect you. I've ordered the guns on my yacht to be trained on this mob."

"He don't have no guns on his yacht!" someone from the white side shouted.

"Think what you will. After war was declared on Spain this spring, the navy outfitted some of our Cape Fear boats with cannons." This seemed to cow the angry men.

Across the dividing line of Water Street, Mr. Sprunt addressed an elderly man in a gray frock coat with a double row of brass buttons down the front. "Colonel Moore, you acted honorably in defending the Confederacy. I beg of you, show the same courage now and stop this senseless terrorizing of my workers."

Someone in the white mob shouted, "If you don't give the order to shoot at the Negroes, we'll do so anyway!"

Colonel Moore turned to face his men and said, "I've been placed in command by my fellow citizens, and until I'm removed from command, I will not allow bloodshed. Any instigators will be arrested. Is this understood?"

Sprunt ordered all his workers back inside. They

stampeded toward the large open doors. I was shorter than the men and was smothered by the forward crush of bodies. I didn't want to be barricaded inside and tried to stop and let others go around me, but I was swept forward. Remembering Daddy's instructions for avoiding being caught in a riptide—don't resist, but let the tide carry you until it loses its power—I gave in and let myself be pushed into the warehouse.

At the far end of the enormous space was a timber structure three stories high. It held the monstrous hydraulic machine that smashed the loose bales of cotton from the gin into denser blocks to be loaded onto foreign-bound vessels. I ran behind a stack of uncompressed bales and located an exit that had not yet been closed off.

I found myself alone on the deserted waterfront, eerie for its lack of bustle. I sprinted along the planks, past schooners and steamers, until I could go no farther. Then I cut over into the neighborhood, walking part of the way, then running. I had to get back to Boo Nanny quick, to warn her to get inside.

Others had the same idea. Negro workers in coveralls poured out of the shipping firms, sawmills, and turpentine plants along the river. The streets, already a cauldron of rumor and fear, were now filled with wild-eyed men desperate to get back to their families.

A gathering of loud white men forced me to go several blocks north before cutting over at Harnett Street. This was a mixed neighborhood and business district on the edge of Darktown, where whites and blacks had always gotten along.

On the southwest corner of Fourth and Harnett, a group of whites had gathered in front of Brunje's Saloon. There were fewer than at Sprunt's—dozens rather than hundreds—but these men seemed more agitated and unruly.

I looked around for cover. Kitty-corner from where I was standing, some thirty Negroes milled about in front of Walker's Grocery, a one-story building with a tarp that extended out from the porch to shade the cabbages, potatoes, and apples stacked on outdoor tables. Our family had a running tab at Walker's. Boo Nanny sent me there for eggs and sugar when we were out.

A burly police officer with a white beard and fat pink cheeks like Santy Claw tried unsuccessfully to get the Negroes to go home. When that didn't work, a black man I knew by sight but not by name attempted to break up the crowd. "In the name of God, for the sake of your lives, your family, your children, and your country, go home," he pleaded.

The men hissed at him. He continued: "I'm as brave

as any of you, but we're unarmed and powerless. Can't you see that?"

Sensing trouble, I slipped under an old wooden boat overturned in Ernest Dockery's front yard, one house west of the corner. Under the boat, I stretched out on the fishing nets and rested my elbows on a coil of rope. The boat was tilted enough so that I could peer out through the gap between the sand and the gunwale. Shivering, I put on the jacket the Love Ladies had given me.

Suddenly a shot rang out—from which direction, I couldn't tell. The Negroes had no weapons. A woman from a house on the other side of the boat screamed, "Billy, a white man's been shot!"

There was a moment of silence, then all hell broke loose. Like Fourth of July fireworks, the air sputtered and spit with noise. Black men broke and ran in all directions, like pigeons released from a plunge trap, with whites firing after them.

One man from the white side shouted, "Shame, men! Stop this! Stop this! Don't you see these dead men?"

"We're just shooting to see the niggers run!" someone said.

A group of black men took off down Harnett Street, followed by a hail of bullets. Some men were driven back toward the railroad, with whites in pursuit. Those who remained at the grocery store hurled potatoes and cabbages at the white men across the street.

A bullet whizzed over the boat, and I rolled back from the edge, terrified. I remained there, shaking uncontrollably, until the firing stopped. Then I crawled out, crouched behind the overturned boat, and looked at the horrible scene.

Blood was everywhere. The dirt street was covered with spent bullets and torn clothing. The splintered, hand-lettered sign from Walker's Grocery lay upended in the sand. Potatoes, cabbages, and apples littered the road. Black bodies lay crumpled and bent into odd shapes, like driftwood scattered on the beach.

A bell started ringing from the steeple of St. Matthew's English Lutheran, the white clapboard church beside Brunje's Saloon. The militia would be here soon. My neighborhood was at war.

It didn't take long for the ambulance from Cowan's Livery Stable to arrive. A freckled young man brought two white horses to a stop at the intersection. The wagon he pulled had a large Red Cross banner on it.

The Negroes had all disappeared, except for the dead and injured. Relatives had hauled off several of the bloodied men, and I saw one man crawl on his stomach, pulling himself by his elbows, the way Lewis and I inched through the underbrush when we played war. The man managed to get himself under a little shotgun house raised on rocks, just north of Walker's Grocery.

By now the white men had reassembled in front of the saloon. Their numbers had swelled, as had the number of weapons.

"Where's the man who was shot?" the young ambulance driver called out.

A white man shouted, "They took him to Moore's Drugstore!"

My heart was beating so hard, I thought I might faint. I wanted to tell the ambulance driver, "Can't you see? Open your eyes! Use your ears!" There were black men writhing and moaning in the street. But I dared not come out from my hiding place to show him the injured men. I was a coward.

One of the white horses raised its tail and dropped a steaming pile onto the street by a crumpled body. The young driver struck the animal's rump with a whip, and the ambulance zigzagged around the bodies and galloped off toward the drugstore, leaving the injured men behind in the sand.

I crawled back under the boat and rolled myself into a ball. If I'd had the guts to approach the ambulance driver instead of cowering behind the boat on top of a stinky fishnet, I could have saved the lives of several wounded men. My insides felt sour. I would never, ever tell anyone about my craven deed. It was my secret shame. I wept, both for my lack of gumption and for the things I had witnessed.

I took a roundabout way home, avoiding the streets and traveling behind houses until I reached the sunken railroad tracks, where Lewis and I had once defended our territory from the white boys. No one would bother me there.

Sure enough, the weedy track was empty. I followed the wooden ties, keeping an ear out for the train whistle. It didn't take long to reach the bridge near my house that crossed over the tracks dividing Darktown from the white neighborhood to the south.

Because the south slope was not as steep, I climbed up that side, burrowing out toeholds in the dirt and pulling myself up by the bushes and vines that clung to the bank. When I reached the top, I immediately realized my mistake. The road was clogged with angry white citizens, brought to a standstill at the narrow mouth of the bridge. There were both civilians and militia—Rough Riders, Red Shirts on horseback, and the Wilmington Light Infantry, all trying to get into my neighborhood at once. Men pushed and shoved to get across. The crowd forced some men up against the shanks of snorting horses, skittish from the crowds. The man driving the Gatling gun stood on the wagon seat and yelled for people to make room for him to pass. No one budged.

Behind me, a boy and his father were trying to cross the bridge. I turned and recognized Tommy. I hadn't seen him since our skinny-dipping caper in the Cape Fear River. His freckles had faded to faint splotches.

With horror, I realized that I was wearing the Love Ladies' jacket, the one with the cinched waist. I was mortified that he would see me in it, even though I wasn't sure, from his blank stare, if he recognized me at all.

Before I could take the jacket off, Tommy passed in front of me. People were jammed so close together that our legs got tangled and I stumbled. "Sorry," Tommy mumbled.

His father jerked him by the shoulder and said, "What's that, boy?"

Tommy looked confused. "I tripped him by mistake," he said.

"But what's that you just said to him?" His father wore a red shirt and had a pistol tucked in his waist-band.

"I said s-s-sorry," he stuttered.

"Are you a half-wit? You don't apologize to a nigger. Ever."

His father was a big man. Tommy looked scared—

more scared than when he had seen the ghost on the railroad tracks.

"I didn't mean it," he said, and it was unclear whether he didn't mean to trip me or didn't mean to apologize.

"Teach him a lesson."

"Let's just keep going," Tommy mumbled. "It don't matter." He didn't look at me, and I dared not look at him. I didn't know if Tommy knew that I had kept his identity a secret and protected him from the police.

"What do you mean it don't matter? He's in your way, you kick him."

"He wasn't. Please. Let's move on." He looked around desperately.

I wanted to return to the way it had been underground, in the pitch black, when our differences didn't matter so much as the fact that we were in a tight spot together, and together we had to get out of it.

His father twirled Tommy around and shoved him in my direction. "You go back and show him who's boss."

Looking down, he gave a little tap to my ankle, barely grazing me.

"That ain't no kick," his father said. "Harder. Act like you mean it."

Tommy looked at me with sad green eyes, fighting back tears. I could tell for sure that he recognized me and remembered everything. We were bound together by secrets: secret gifts, the secret tunnel, a secret friendship. And now this final secret: he didn't want to kick me. Of this I was certain. As certain as anything I knew in my life. But his father towered above him, and Tommy was shaking. He had no choice. With his chin tucked on his chest, he cocked back his leg and let it fly. The pain shot up my shin.

"Atta boy. That'll teach him," his father said.

It wasn't the welt that smarted so badly. What hurt was something that wouldn't go away as quickly.

I broke sideways through the crowd. When I reached the edge of the drop to the railroad tracks, I leaned over and emptied the contents of my stomach into the weeds. I felt humiliated and deeply, deeply sorry, whether for myself or Tommy, I couldn't say.

When I finally got across the bridge, I was in familiar territory but I felt no safer. The Negroes had fled from the streets in terror, leaving only armed white men. An alarming number carried axes, as if the lumberjacks from the pine barrens had been called into service.

I passed by the house of one of the shut-ins from Boo Nanny's church. I saw two men reduce her front door to splinters. The elderly widow was hard of hearing and couldn't walk without a cane. I sometimes brought her groceries.

White men suspected everyone of harboring weapons, even the churches. I glanced down the block to the Baptist church. The Gatling gun that had been ahead of me on the bridge was now aimed at the entrance to the church. Navy Reserve members in crisp white uniforms were lined up across the street, rifles pointed. I had to get home quickly. Nothing was safe, not even the churches.

The day had turned gray and heavy. I scurried along with my head down, not wanting to call attention to myself. I would have cut through the backyards, but the Holloways had a mean dog and a broken-down fence, and I didn't want to chance it. Instead, I moved over to the median that divided Fifth Street—a sandy strip lined with live oaks drooping with kinky gray haint's hair.

From up ahead, I heard a terrible shrieking. I didn't know whether to go toward the cries or away. I continued and soon came upon a little girl leaning against an oak. She had braids all over her head, each tied with a pink ribbon, and looked to be about seven. The lower part of her arm, from the wrist to the elbow, had been split open by a bayonet. The gaping wound made me think of the inside of a pomegranate with the shiny red seeds. For such a little girl, she made a big noise, and the armed men had cleared away from her.

I tried to quiet her down and get her to tell me her name, but all she could do was wail "Mama."

"I'm not your mama, but I'll get you fixed up. Don't you worry," I said.

I knew I had to save her. It was the only way I could make up for what I had done earlier, when I let the ambulance drive away from the wounded men.

We were three-quarters of a mile from the hospital but only a few blocks from my house, so I decided to take her there. I looked around for help. The Negroes had cleared off the streets, but after going down an alley, I was able to round up a thin, middle-aged woman and an unshaven man with grizzled white growth on his face, like frost on a nut.

Luckily, the old man seemed to know what to do. "Take off your shirt," he instructed me. I did, and he bit into the tail, ripped a strip off the bottom, and tied it around the little girl's arm above the wound, like the tail on a kite. Then he knotted the arms of my shirt around a branch to make a flag.

I found a wood plank in a nearby yard. We put the little girl on it, and I covered her with the Love Ladies' jacket. I took the front of the plank, the grandfather took the back, and the woman walked along beside us, waving my sooty white shirt to give us free passage.

The little girl left a trail of blood and little pink bows. Her cries petered out into hiccup-like gasps, each one shorter than the next, until finally they stopped altogether. As much as I welcomed the pause in her screaming, the silence made me more nervous. Noise meant life.

By this time, there were sentinels on every block, but no one stopped us. We got her to my house and placed her on the low kitchen table. I was afraid the girl was dead. The grandfather and the woman who helped me must have thought the same thing, for they fled like fleas from a dead dog. Boo Nanny felt the girl's forehead and pulse and pronounced her puny but alive.

My faith in Boo Nanny's potions had weakened of late, but now I prayed that I had underestimated her healing powers, as I followed her into her library of medicinal herbs. There were no labels, but she knew exactly what she wanted and pulled down three jars of dried leaves.

Her hands full, she said, "Now git that shine in the Mason jar by my bed."

She had moonshine in her room? This was the first I'd heard about it.

"Wipe that look off you face. They's a thing or two you don't know 'bout me," she said.

In the kitchen, I spoon-fed the little girl clear

moonshine while Boo Nanny pounded the herbs with a mortar and pestle.

"We got us a strong one," Boo Nanny said after the girl stopped crying. "That chile's got gumption. Now get youself over here and lend a hand."

She gave me a dented tin cup. "Fill that to the first knuckle of your pointing finger with this," she said, and gave me a jar. "Then add a pinch of this." She pushed another jar my way.

"Is this right?" I was afraid I would get the jars reversed. "What if I mess up?" I said.

"You ain't gone mess up, Cocoa Baby."

She emptied the herbs into a cast-iron pot, then added some other ingredients to make a paste the color of a wasp's nest. I stood over the stove and stirred the foul-smelling concoction in one direction only, just like Boo Nanny said. After it cooled, she dabbed it on the child's wound, then bound her arm with clean cloths.

While the little girl rested quietly under a blanket on the cot that we had moved into the kitchen, Boo Nanny cleaned up. The table was a mess, like the work space at the fish market after the day's catch was gutted and cleaned. Boo Nanny swabbed down the table and scrubbed it with baking soda.

I felt relieved that the potion had stopped the bleeding, and was certain that everything would be okay. But Boo Nanny declared that we needed to get the little girl to the hospital at once. She had lost too much blood.

I didn't have time to wash, but I put on a fresh shirt and grabbed another jacket. Just as I was ready to start out for the hospital, the sound of gunfire came from the direction of the dance hall, the ramshackle gray-board shack two blocks east. On weekends the place was packed with sinners, or so Boo Nanny said when she forbade me to go near it. But on summer nights, notes of the ragtime piano floated down the block through my open window, and sin never sounded so sweet. Now the pop and sputter of guns stood between me and the hospital.

While I waited for the streets to quiet down, the little girl came in and out of consciousness, wheezing and whimpering like a puppy, then falling silent. I didn't leave her side. She was my special charge. I wanted to keep her awake, and thought of telling her one of Boo Nanny's ghost stories—I knew them all by heart—but those stories only worked when you could thrill to the sensation of being pretend-scared. This was the real thing.

By the time calm returned to the streets, a cold drizzle had started to fall. I put the little girl inside a wheelbarrow, wrapped her in a blanket, and placed an oilcloth on top to protect her from the rain. She was totally covered, except for her pigtails, which stuck out like the spikes of a sea urchin. She was peaceful and breathing evenly.

There was no easy way to get to the hospital, which was to the east, in the direction of the dance hall. I turned my wheelbarrow around and took the longer route.

It was late afternoon, and darkness was fast approaching. On the way I passed a straggling line of Negroes—mainly women and children—headed toward the cypress swamp. They lugged bundles of bedding and clothes. Some children huddled under tarps they held over their heads against the rain, while others shivered in their wet coats. Mothers hushed their wailing babies and hurried the children along in the grim mist, all headed toward a nighttime of uncertainty.

Lewis and I rarely played in the swamp, especially not in winter. It was too miserable. I wondered if these poor people knew what awaited them: sloshing calf-deep in icy-cold water through the brooding dark, with snakes hiding in the thick vines overhead and the underwater roots and jutting knees of the cypresses slimy with decay, ready to trip up the youngest and nimblest among them. But even this horror was preferable to staying in town. Who could say if they were making the right choice?

I pushed the little girl in the wheelbarrow several blocks before a sentry stopped me.

"What are you transporting?" he said.

"A wounded girl. We're on the way to the hospital."

The militia man cast aside the oilcloth and roughly removed the blanket I had so carefully wrapped around my charge. The little girl cried out in pain.

"You're hurting her," I protested.

"Got to check for weapons," he said.

I reached the Negro hospital, a one-story clapboard building the size of a church sanctuary. It was connected to the rear of City Hospital by a passageway with open sides. In the back, a horrible sight awaited me. The newly arrived wounded spilled over into the yard. Negroes lay on litters in the rain, as nurses rushed to take names and separate the wounded into groups according to how serious their injuries were. Frantic women searched the stretchers for husbands, brothers, and sons. The sounds of wailing and moaning surrounded me, and screams came from the hospital, as if we were in the loony bin.

Someone had tied a makeshift tarp between trees in an attempt to keep the rain off. A woman stood beside a stretcher underneath and cried out for a sedative for her husband.

"We ain't got enough. We can't even buy whiskey. The ban from the election's still in place," a nurse said. Her damp white hat rested atop her twiggy hair like a dove on a nest.

"Can't you get some from the main hospital?" the desperate woman asked.

The nurse snorted, then turned away to attend to a grandmother who clawed at the open wound in her side with bent fingers.

I found another nurse who was circulating and pleaded my case. "She's lost a lot of blood. I need to get her help immediately," I said. The little girl was now quiet, just when I needed her to be loud.

"You and everybody else, sweetie."

"But she's a little girl. Can't she go inside?"

"Full. We don't have room."

Finally the nurse agreed to take us to the passageway between the white and black hospitals. I parked the wheelbarrow there, alongside other people—some on stretchers, some sitting on the floor, others on pallets of old blankets. At least we were out of the rain. There was no traffic, no doctors from the white hospital coming to pitch in.

At the end of the passageway, I saw Dr. Hudson, our

family doctor, who had been at the meeting at Jacobs's barbershop the previous night. I was so happy to see a familiar face. "Dr. Hudson! Dr. Hudson!" I shouted, but he couldn't hear me above the din of crying patients.

I ran up to him and said, "You've got to help me. I've got a little girl who's hurt bad."

"Son, we've got more injured than we know what to do with. We're short of everything—blood, doctors, nurses. I've never seen anything like it."

"Please," I begged.

"I'll do what I can," he said.

True to his word, he soon sent a nurse to find me. Looking at the bundle in the wheelbarrow, then at her clipboard, she said gruffly, "Name?"

I panicked. If I said I didn't know, she might not help us. "Hope," I said. "Hope Thomas."

The name popped out. I didn't know where it came from. But that was what I needed at the moment. That was what I longed for, and somehow, that was what the little girl meant to me.

"T-H-O-M-A-S." I spelled it out, anxious for the nurse to get her on paper, to make it official.

"You can leave her here. She'll be in good hands," the nurse said.

When I got home, Boo Nanny heated water on the

stove and filled up a large galvanized tin, large enough to be baptized in. She left me in privacy to take a bath.

I was exhausted and numb, but I felt jubilant. I had rescued Hope. On a day filled with unspeakable acts, I had done a good deed. It wasn't much, but it was a start.

THIRTEEN

As the sun set, the streets quieted down, but still we had no word from Mama or Daddy. Darkness brought a whole new set of fears. After my bath, Boo Nanny made me help her peel potatoes to keep me occupied while we waited.

Mama arrived first, and we crowded around and hugged her. She had been stopped several times on the way home from work, but the Red Shirts had let her through.

Boo Nanny suggested supper, but Mama said, "I ain't gone eat till I know Jack's all right. Let's wait a bit longer."

She played hymns on the organ to pass the time.

After what seemed like a long while, Daddy appeared at the back door. His white shirt was smudged with soot, his jacket was torn, and his eyes were shot through with wiggly red lines.

Mom pulled him close, not caring a wit that she got ash all over her dress.

I waited my turn. He put his hand on my head and said, "Moses, you made me proud today." He didn't know about the injured men I could have pointed out to the ambulance driver and didn't. His praise was undeserved, but it still made me happy.

He had spent his day sifting through the charred remains of the *Record*. Almost nothing was left. What had not burned was ruined by water. "Now's the time our community really needs a paper to make sense of what's going on. But it's destroyed, along with all of the back issues. I can't stand to think about it—the voice of the people silenced, the historical record wiped out." He choked back tears. But he wouldn't be Daddy if he didn't look on the bright side. "At least none of our employees was killed. For that, I'm grateful."

I wanted all this trouble behind us, so we could get back to the way things were before.

We sat down to supper, and Boo Nanny gave the blessing. Sometimes she could get creative, but tonight she was straightforward: "We is together and we is safe, and ain't none of us gone get greedy and ask for more than that, so thankee, Lord. Amen."

Even Daddy, who wasn't a believer, seemed to draw comfort from her words.

It was so late by the time we finished supper that everyone went straight to bed. Sometime in the night, I was awoken by a strange sound. Chills tingled along my spine. The sound came again: a long, low whistle that definitely was not a bird. Soon there was an angry rapping at the door.

I padded down the back hall in the dark.

"Stay here," Daddy said, passing by me. He was wearing a red union suit.

I stood by the back hall door and looked into the parlor.

"Who goes there?" Daddy said.

"White men. Only white men."

"What do you want?"

"Open, or we'll take the door by force."

Daddy opened the door, and half a dozen armed men came into the parlor. Two carried lanterns. The men wore red shirts or pieces of military uniforms. It was the most white people that had ever been in our house at one time.

"Your presence is no longer desired in this city. We've reached a compromise. We have purchased you a one-way ticket to Richmond. You will go and not return," said the bald man holding the lantern. The light cast dark shadows in the hollows where his eyes were, giving him the look of a skull.

"That is not a compromise. That is a one-sided proposition, which is the exact opposite of a compromise," Daddy said.

"We ain't here for an English lesson from the likes of you," said one of the Red Shirts.

I huddled in the dark, terrified. Mama came up behind me and put her arms around me. Boo Nanny peered through a crack in her door.

"I am a husband and father. My family depends on me as the main wage earner. By what rights can you ban me from my city?" Daddy said.

It was strange to see him in his red union suit, standing in a room of Red Shirts.

"It was a unanimous decision by the Committee of Twenty-Five," said the bald man.

"I see you hold democracy in high regard for members of your own race. If there's a unanimous vote by a self-selected group that supports your purpose, you're all for it. But if the citizens express themselves legally through elections and you don't like the results, then you feel justified in overturning the will of the people."

While he talked, several of the men surveyed the organ, the curio cabinet, the horsehair sofa, examining each object as if ready to make a bid. One man opened the wooden box on the side table and took out the program that the Siamese twins had signed for Mama.

"I'll thank you to put that back," Daddy said firmly.

"We're here to take you to the county jail," the bald man said.

Mama gave a little gasp, and I was afraid the others had heard her, but no one looked our way.

"Jail? On what grounds?" Daddy said.

"It's for your own protection. You should be grateful. There are angry men out there itching for a lynching bee."

"I don't need your brand of protection."

"I'm afraid you don't have a choice. You can come with us peacefully, or we will take you by force."

My heart was working so hard I was afraid it would break out of my chest and gallop across the room. I felt Mama's arms tighten around me.

"What crime have I committed? What transgression so grave that I be hunted down in my own home and banished from this city I love? State it, please, so that I may defend myself. In our democratic system, we have courts, judges, and juries for that purpose."

The men looked at one another. For a moment I thought he might have changed some minds.

He continued: "Let's be clear. This is not about your protecting me or protecting the community. This is about mob rule, a white minority that has seized control of a city and thrown out the rule of law, along with the democratically elected city government. Mark my words, this will not stand the scrutiny of time." His voice cracked, and he coughed to cover it up.

A young boy in a red shirt started to sweat and breathe heavily. He was not much older than me.

"Go outside and wait for us there," one of the older men told him, then turned back to Daddy. "We come with our heads held high, to take you for your own safety."

"And in so doing, do you claim to be more virtuous than if you were covered with white robes?"

"We got ourselves a silver-tongued Sambo here. Are you going to take this from him?" said one of the Red Shirts.

"This will shut him up," said a man in a khaki Rough Riders tunic. The pistol in his hand went *click, click, click.*

Daddy waited a moment, then took a deep breath. "I will cooperate with you, because I see that I don't have a choice and because I don't want to expose my family to any more trauma. Since you are hell-bent on denying me any shred of dignity, I will take it for myself. You will allow me a few private words with my family. I will be in the back bedroom."

Surprisingly, they granted him his wish.

I followed him to the bedroom. No one spoke as he

solemnly put on pants, a freshly laundered shirt, and the shoes he had shined before going to bed. His hands were shaking so badly that when he tried to attach the shirt collar, it slipped from his hand and landed on the dresser with a soft thud. Mama picked it up and tenderly helped him.

After he finished dressing and packing his bag, he sat on the bed and called me over to him. With both hands resting on my shoulders, he looked directly at me. "Always remember, you are the equal of every man, and every man is your equal."

Tears gathered in my eyes.

"I want you to take care of your mother and grandmother until I return. Will you do that for me?" Daddy asked. I nodded solemnly. "I'll be back as soon as I can. You have my word on that, and you know what store I set by my word."

He took out Grandpa Tip's gold watch and put it in my hand. "I want you to hold this for me for safekeeping."

I closed my palm around the watch that he had promised to give me when I graduated from college. He lifted my chin. "No tears," he said, and wiped the corners of his own eyes. "Now, son, give me a few private moments with your mother."

I went to my room and put the gold watch in a box

with my other treasures. The county jail was a mere five blocks away. If I slipped out and ran to the jail, I would get there before he did. I raised the window and leaped from the sill, aiming wide to clear the rosebush.

"Halt!"

There were two Red Shirts stationed outside. I heard the click of a gun.

"Wait! It's a boy," someone cried. I picked myself up off the sand and raised my hands.

"Oh, God!" It was the Red Shirt youngster who had been in the parlor. He threw his gun onto the sand and staggered back into the magnolia tree. The thick leathery leaves clapped against one another. He bent over, put his hands on his knees, and gasped for breath, as if coming up for air after being underwater too long. The older man tried to calm him. It was only then that I realized how close I had come to getting shot.

Daddy walked out the front door, head up, back erect, and climbed into the wagon. He didn't see me in the side yard. The two Red Shirts left me and joined the men posted on the other sides of the house. They all piled into the wagon with Daddy, and the horse clopped off.

I tried to pull myself together. I couldn't be weak at a time like this. Mama needed me. I was the man of the house now.

• • •

Boo Nanny, Mama, and I slept in the same bed that night, but no one got much sleep. Early the next morning, we all went to the county jail on Princess Street. Outside it was chilly and damp, but the sun shone brightly and the sky was fresh and clean, the way it is after a rain.

On the way, we passed a tree where someone had hung two sepia photographs in gold frames, the glass cracked across the faces. The male portrait was tagged R. H. BUNTING—WHITE. Under the woman's portrait were the words MRS. R. H. BUNTING—COLORED. Mama turned my head away, grabbed my elbow, and hurried me past.

We joined the people milling outside the jailhouse. From overheard snippets of conversation, I learned that a number of Wilmington's Negro citizens had spent the night in jail and would be escorted to the train station in time for the 9:10.

"Miss Ellen ain't gone like this one bit, but I'm gone be late for work," Mama said.

"You gone get youself fired, pure and simple," Boo Nanny said.

"I'll find more work. White folk thinks we so dangerous, yet they lets us take care of their babies. What sense do that make?"

I flipped open Grandpa Tip's gold watch. I had put it

in my pocket for good luck. It was 8:22 train time. I closed the lid, with the teeth marks. More than anything about the watch, I loved those dents.

At quarter to nine, half a dozen Negroes emerged from the jail, each escorted by two soldiers carrying rifles with bayonets. I recognized most of the men. They were prominent members of the black community. Despite the proclamations of wanting to rid the Port City of ignorant Negroes, it was the educated, successful blacks who were chosen for exile.

Armed members of the Wilmington Light Infantry had spaced themselves along the route to the railroad station. White people lined the streets as if for a parade.

I had an ugly feeling in my stomach as I watched Lewis's proud father being kicked and prodded along the corridor by two armed men. Hoodlums jeered and shouted from the roadside.

Daddy was last in line. His posture was so slumped, I almost didn't recognize him. He must have slept in his suit, for he looked rumpled and unkempt. Even his shoes had lost their shine. He walked between the two soldiers in small, shuffling steps. His eyes were blank, focused on the ground in front of him.

I ran behind the spectators, jumping up at intervals and shouting "Daddy! Daddy!" to catch his attention.

He couldn't hear me over the chorus of "Dixie" that had broken out from the sidelines.

I ran faster to get in front of him. People glared at me, but I didn't care. Closer to the train station, I edged my way to the front row, squatted down, and waited for the sad procession of Negroes to reach me.

When I saw Daddy, I sprang up and called to him. Finally I was able to make myself heard above the commotion. When he saw me, the spark returned to his eyes and he smiled. Then he straightened his back, raised his head high, and marched forward, his dignity restored.

The train was waiting at the station. I looked around in the crowd for Mama and Boo Nanny. Seagulls squawked overhead, and the air smelled of fish. The tip of a schooner's mast on the Cape Fear was visible over the roof of the station.

The soldiers led the Negroes to the back of the train. Farther up the platform, porters were carrying luggage. I put my hand in my pocket and felt the gold watch ticking against my palm. I prayed that Grandpa Tip was not working as a porter that day so he would be spared this sight.

The Negroes entered the train one by one. There were no porters to bring the box to make it easier to reach the bottom rung of the train steps. The men struggled to climb up. Daddy helped push the elderly preacher up the steps, then pulled himself up, the last in line. At the top, he paused and turned to address the crowd.

"The white supremacists among you decry black crime and black laziness, but it is, in truth, black competence and independence that you fear most. Witness here the men you have chosen to banish."

From the crowd came shouts of "Who gave him the right to speak?" "Cocky!" "Uppity!" "Impudent!"

The soldier beside him tried to push him inside, but he resisted.

I closed my eyes tight against the brightness of the sun and repeated silently, *Get inside. Get into the car right now.*

The whistle sounded, and the porter came by ringing a bell. The train was ready to pull out of the station.

Mama found me in the crowd and came up beside me. "Make him hush up, Mama," I whispered.

But Daddy would not be silenced. He continued: "These men are not minstrels, buffoons, or faithful retainers. Those types pose no threat. No, these men are educated, ambitious achievers—preachers, lawyers, men who own businesses and homes. *That* is what scares you."

"Jack!" Mama cried out, and raised her hand so Daddy could see her. I felt my heart lift. She would make him stop talking. She was the only one who could.

She pushed through the spectators. When she got to the front row, a Red Shirt said, "Get back there, you little high yaller hussy," and shoved her hard with the butt of his rifle.

She cried out in pain and crumpled onto the platform thirty feet from the train.

Daddy saw it happen. "Sadie!" he cried, and leaped off the steps to help her.

"He's escaping!" came a shout from the crowd.

A shot rang out. Daddy slumped over on the platform. My heart went cold.

Mama got to her feet, and we raced to his side. Mama cradled his head in her lap, and I held his hand.

"Somebody get help!" she cried frantically. Daddy had a large opening in his neck.

Boo Nanny reached us. She took off her shawl and mopped up the blood.

The doors to the railway car closed. I felt a hot blast of steam from under the train as it chugged out of the station. A shrill rebel yell broke through the air. The Red Shirts backed the spectators away to leave space around us.

Mama rubbed Daddy's temples. "Baby, we here. We always here." Her lap was wet and red.

My mind was racing. *I should know what to do.* I had practice in this sort of thing. I had saved the little girl.

Surely I could save my own daddy. But blood was running out so fast. If I tied the shawl around his neck to stop the flow, he'd choke.

"Daddy, tell me what to do. I'll do anything."

"Never . . ." His voice was a whisper. The clank of the wheels made it hard to hear.

I put my ear closer to his chapped lips. "What, Daddy?"

"Never give up. Always . . ."

"Always what?" I was desperate. The crowd broke out in cheers and yells as the train left the station.

I felt him grip my hand harder as he tried to lift his head off Mama's lap. "Always . . . ," he whispered, straining toward me. Then his head slumped to the side and his handshake went limp.

A small group followed the pine casket through the scrub oak and wire grass, over paths covered with fingertip-sized acorns that, when squashed, revealed a pumpkin-colored interior.

All around the cemetery, people had cordoned off small squares with stakes and string. There were so many fresh mounds of dirt, the land looked like a building site.

We buried Daddy beneath a buzzard-free sky. As we sang "Safe in the Arms of Jesus," Mama looked nervously around her. Three days after the riots, it was still not safe for groups of Negroes to gather together. After a brief service, we left.

I wanted to remember the good things about Daddy, but every time I thought of him, I saw that hole in his neck, his cracked lips, the red stain on Mama's skirt, so wide and dark that rather than turn the skirt over to Boo Nanny for washing, she burned it in the backyard pit.

During the days that followed, many people came up to me and told me that my daddy was a hero. But I didn't want a hero. I wanted a father. I loved Boo Nanny and Mama with all my heart, but who would teach me how to be a man?

Several weeks later, when I visited Daddy's grave, I found it covered with objects. Friends and neighbors who were too scared to attend the funeral had crept back when no one was looking to leave something on his grave. Almost every object was damaged in some way, broken, rusted, melted, burned. Some things could only have come from the men at the *Record*: lead printing-press letters fused together in a clump, a mangled typewriter, its innards melted. Other objects must have meant something to the giver: a toy horse with a yarn mane, an ax handle without the head, a pine box that once held Borax, a rusted snuff tin, a hearing horn, a mouth organ, a biscuit cutter—simple, everyday objects placed there as a kind of tribute.

I sat at the foot of my father's grave and wept.

I thought of the time I left little presents in the crook of the tree by the swimming hole for Tommy. It had felt good. That was why I did it. I enjoyed getting the gifts he left for me, but even more, I liked thinking up things to give him.

I tried to picture Daddy's face, but I couldn't. At least not now. But that didn't mean he was gone. Far from it.

I never told anyone this—they might have hauled me off to the Asylum for the Colored Insane in Goldsboro if I did—but Daddy was not dead. Rather, he had taken on a different form. Not like Boo Nanny's haints, who roamed the earth causing mischief. He stayed closer to home. Over the years, I would grow bigger, but he would stay the same: something small and light and precious that I carried inside me. I would keep him safe, always.

FOURTEEN

Christmas passed in a blur. The New Year was no better. Mama lost her job with the Gilchrists. At first she didn't seem to mind. "It'll do that baby child good to be with his real mama for a change," she said, referring to the Gilchrists' three-year-old son, Edward. But when she couldn't find a place anywhere else, she started to wear down.

When I announced that I was quitting school to find a job, she said, "I don't care if we gots to live on acorns and seaweed. You ain't quittin' school, no way, so don't even think about it. You is gone finish high school, then you is gone go to college, and after that, I don't know what you is gone do, but it's gone be something good, 'cause you is your daddy's boy."

A white family bought Lewis's fine house when he and his family moved up North. His father was forced to sell off the bank and his other properties at fire-sale prices. Before leaving, Lewis gave me his marble collection for safekeeping, though I think we both knew he would never come back. I kept the marbles in a Mason jar on my windowsill, but they were no replacement for a friend.

One day at the end of February, I found Boo Nanny on the back steps, rocking and moaning.

"What's wrong?"

"I got de miseries in my back," she said, picking at her skirt. Her clawed hands were dark with lye burns.

I was alarmed. She was overworked. Mama helped with the laundry when she wasn't out looking for work or doing odd jobs here and there, and I helped after school. But the burden fell mostly on Boo Nanny.

"What can I do?" I hated to see her in pain like that.

"Ain't you something, Cocoa Baby, worrying 'bout these old bones. Give me a moment and I'll be pert like usual."

"What's to become of us?" I asked.

"Sounds to me like you got youself a powerful case of the sorries. That'll wear you down quicker'n anything," she said. "I seed worse days than this, and I's here to tell you, we might be in for a right smart spell, but we gone bear what we got to and we gone get by just fine long as we be thankful for what we got, and not sniffling over what we ain't got."

. . .

The call of the bull alligator announced the beginning
of spring. Grass appeared in the low grounds along the
river, and chestnuts disappeared from the city markets,
along with sweet-en-taters, possum, and sides of veni-
son. Soon spring was full upon us, with waves of sweet
smells and bright mornings.

Mama still had not found a job, and Boo Nanny's
work was spotty. If Lewis's father had still owned the
bank, he would have allowed us to delay house payments for several months, but the new owners wouldn't
work with us, and we were close to losing the house. We
had already auctioned off most of the parlor furniture,
but Mama had put off selling the organ. Now there was
no choice. Money from the sale would allow us to limp
along for a few more months until we got on our feet.

I volunteered to go back to the clock repairman who
sold us the organ to see if he would buy it back. The
small shop on Front Street was crammed with clocks of
all shapes and sizes. All were set to the same time, except
for the ones by his worktable in need of repair. A grandfather clock stood by the front door. A glass case held
trays of pocket watches, some waiting for pickup, others
for sale.

The man was stooped over a worktable by the window with tweezers in his hand and a loupe in his right

eye. Watch parts were spread out on the table—screws, springs, and disks of various sizes, some with toothed edges and others with rims and spokes, all tiny.

When the man looked up from his work, I described the organ we had purchased from him and asked if he would be interested in buying it back.

"Oh, yes, I remember." He removed the loupe from his eye and set it on his forehead. "I'll give you thirty," he said.

"Thirty dollars?" I said, unsure I had understood him.

"Correct."

"We paid a hundred less than a year ago."

"I doubt it."

I would know. For a solid year I had stashed away two one-dollar bills a week in the pages of the dictionary. I would never forget Mama's face when she clapped her eyes on the organ for the first time. I might never see that much joy in her face again, which made me sad. But those were different times. Now we needed the money more than the organ. "No, I remember clearly. We paid a hundred," I said.

"Well, that wasn't very smart of you."

Either he had cheated us on the original price or he was trying to cheat me now. "What will you take?" I said.

"I've stated my price," he said.

"I can't sell it for that." Suddenly I felt bold. The fact that he was acting shifty reinforced my resolve.

"It ain't worth forty. No one will give that for it. Thirty's my offer. Better take it now while I'm in a generous mood."

As if to tempt me, he took out a roll of bills and started counting them. "You could use the money, couldn't you?" he said, ruffling the end of the stack.

I paused and thought how to respond. I remembered what my father had said about that Dry Ponder when I had mistakenly stolen the bicycle I thought belonged to Lewis: *What he is has nothing to do with what you are.* I would not lie.

"That's not the problem," I said.

"Well then, what is the problem?"

"We aren't even close on the terms." I thought of my grandfather's gold watch and vowed that I would starve before I sold it to this crook.

"Think you're fancy folk, don't you?"

"We are neither smart nor fancy; we are fair."

He straightened his back. "What do you mean by that?"

"Only that thirty is not a fair price, and I won't accept it."

"You think you can just sell it anywhere? You're in for a big surprise."

I thought for a moment. If I didn't sell the organ here, I had no idea where I would sell it. No one in Darktown could afford an organ, and white people would be too afraid to come to our house to look at it. I was throwing away the only chance I had. Thirty dollars was better than nothing. The momentary feeling of bravado left me, and I was ready to accept his offer.

At that moment, the hour of eleven arrived, and dozens of clocks in the store struck the hour in unison. The room filled with pings, gongs, and chimes—a glorious cacophony. Yes, *cacophony*. A big word. A challenge word. I was the keeper of the dictionary now that Daddy was gone.

I could feel my father's presence in the room, could hear him say: *This is how it starts. One small step, and you ignore what you know to be right, and then the next time, it is easier to do, and the next time, a little easier still, and before you know it, every ounce of your self-worth is gone.* No, I would not give in to this man. Not with Jack for a father.

"Thank you for your time," I said when the chimes had run their course. I threw back my shoulders and walked toward the door.

"Now wait a minute, here," he said. "Wait just a minute. I may have some leeway. Would you take sixty?"

I turned around. "No, sir, I would not."

"What about seventy? That's my last offer."

"I understand. But I can't sell for that."

"You're a stubborn little Sambo. Well, give me your best price."

I calculated in my head. I knew this was my last chance, and I didn't want to ruin it by being greedy. I shut my eyes and said, "Eighty-five."

"I'll meet your price, if you will take care of delivery."

"It's a deal." I looked him straight in the eye and gave him a handshake—a firm Jack Thomas handshake.

The first full moon of May marked the beginning of soft-shell crab season. There was a limited time after the blue crabs shed their shells when I could catch Mama and Boo Nanny's favorite food. I didn't have much experience crabbing, but since life had been so hard for us recently, I was determined to provide them with this special treat. At low tide, I took a pole, a net, bait, and a bucket to the salt marsh.

Blue periwinkle shells clung to the roots of the exposed marsh grasses, and fiddler crab holes pocked the mud. Around the edges of the sandbars, purplish clams shone through the muck. I carefully made my way forward, stepping on the roots to avoid sinking.

I tied a chicken neck to a string and tossed it into the water. When I felt a tug, I patiently pulled the bait back, coaxing the crab along until I could scoop it up in my net. After an hour, I had caught five blues, but not a single soft-shell.

I wasn't worried. With the blue sky above and the breeze on my face—warm but not too hot—it was a perfect day. The red shoulders of the blackbirds dotted the marsh grass like cherries. A blue heron took flight, stretching its stilt-like legs awkwardly behind, then tucking them underneath. Above, a circling hawk dove straight down, landing with a splash and coming up with breakfast. All this would change next week, when school ended and I had to find a job. But for this one day, I took in the dizzying joy of complete freedom.

Behind me, I heard sloshing, and then someone called my name. I turned and there was Tommy, his red hair flaming in the sun.

"Hey," I said, and looked down. He was the last person I wanted to meet out here. I hadn't seen him since the day he kicked me.

"How are you?" he said. His cheeks were red and spotted, like pinto beans.

"Okay, I guess."

"Catch yourself any busters?" he said.

"No luck," I said, ashamed to admit that my bucket was filled with hard-shell crabs. They would be good eating, but a lot more work, since we'd have to crack the shell and claws and pick out the meat.

Tommy looked inside my bucket. "You got yourself a red-liner there. She'll drop her shell in a couple of hours," he said.

"How can you tell?"

"See the line along the edge of the back flippers? It's turned from white to red. She's ready to molt, sure enough."

Clearly he knew more than I did. I wanted in the worst way to get away from him, but there was nowhere to go.

"I can show you how to bring along the red-liners till they drop their shells."

"That's okay." He could tell I didn't know what I was doing, and that made me feel worse.

"I been doing this since I was six. It ain't hard," he said.

My ankles tickled as a school of minnows flitted by, wrinkling the surface of the water.

"See that trotline over there?" he said, pointing to the east. I had noticed the bobbing white buoys before but mistook them for gulls. A trotline required more skill but worked much better. A line was stretched between two buoys and baited every two feet or so. "Want to help me run it?"

I looked down without answering. Why wouldn't he leave me alone?

"I'll let you in on a secret, but you got to promise not to tell," he said.

I shrugged.

"Know why the crabbing's better over there?" he said.

He was about to give up a prize piece of information. No waterman worth his salt gave away his secret spots.

"The ones without shells are weak and need a place to hide. That's why they go over there. A sunken boat."

"No kidding." I couldn't hide my glee. "Like a schooner?"

"It's just an old skiff, but enough to give the crabs shelter."

Of course, the marsh was too shallow for the big-masted ships. I felt stupid, but Tommy didn't seem to notice.

"I'll go halves," he said.

I swallowed hard. He could get several bucketfuls, easy, with enough left over to sell at market. I could be out here for hours and not catch a single soft-shell crab. "Naw, I'm not interested," I said.

"Come on, I could use the help."

He kicked the edge of the water and sent a spray that hit me square in the face. It caught me by surprise. I scooped up some water in both hands and slung it toward him. Before long, we were horsing around, splashing each other any way we could. We were already muddy and tired and wet, but the game made us forget all that. The sun turned the sprays of water into tiny rainbows, like the big arcs in the sky, but smaller, filled with all the different colors.

Historical Note

Crow is a novel that combines fictional characters with real historical events. In 1898, four of the ten aldermen in Wilmington, North Carolina, were black, but Jack Thomas is an invented character. Moses, Boo Nanny, Mama, Lewis, and Tommy exist only in my imagination—and now, I hope, in yours as well.

The black Siamese twins Millie-Christine are based on real people. They became a European sensation, performed for the Queen of England, and were so successful that they were able to buy the plantation in Columbus County, North Carolina, where they were born into slavery.

Alex Manly was the real editor of the Wilmington *Daily Record*, the largest black daily in the South. There are several versions of the story of his escape. The one in the novel is fictional, though I took some details from existing accounts.

Many of the minor characters are based on historical figures: John Dancy, appointed collector of customs for the Port of Wilmington by President William McKinley; James Sprunt, owner of the Sprunt Cotton Compress; the Red Shirts; Crazy Drake; Alfred Waddell; and many others.

The tunnels under Wilmington's streets exist today, though for reasons of safety, no one is allowed to go through them.

Many events in the novel are historical, and I wrote them with as much accuracy as research allowed: the white supremacy rally in Fayetteville, the Committee of Twenty-Five's ultimatum to the black citizens, the two-thousand-man march on the *Record* led by Alfred Waddell, the mob's burning of the *Record*, the standoff outside the Sprunt Cotton Compress, and the violence at the corner of Harnett and Fourth Streets.

Where possible, I quoted word for word from speeches and documents, including Alex Manly's editorial; Alfred Waddell's speech in front of Thalian Hall, where he threatened to "choke the Cape Fear River with carcasses"; and the White Declaration of Independence. For purposes of the story, I combined several speeches for the Fayetteville rally and Alfred Waddell's address.

I tried to use language of the time. To that end, I never referred to blacks as African Americans—that term didn't exist in 1898. Instead, I used *Negro* and *colored*, which were respectable words at the time. *Nigger* was then, and is now, a derogatory word. I used it only in the mouths of white supremacists or characters who meant to shock and offend.

The 1898 race riot and coup d'état had a profound impact on race relations in North Carolina and the South. Between 1892 and 1898, eastern North Carolina elected four African American representatives to the U.S. Congress, but not a single one was elected in the entire twentieth century. Wilmington's black middle class was destroyed. In addition to the men who were marched to the train and thrown out of town, many other black leaders were banished, along with whites who were sympathetic to the black cause. Thousands of black citizens fled. Those who owned homes and businesses sold them at fire-sale prices.

After the riot, the newly installed Board of Aldermen appointed Alfred Waddell mayor. Integrated neighborhoods in Wilmington disappeared, and the Jim Crow laws that cemented segregation blossomed. In 1899, signs announcing WHITES ONLY or FOR COLORED popped up at water fountains, bathrooms, restaurants, and theaters across North Carolina. Courtrooms even had separate Bibles to use for swearing in witnesses.

One of the key men behind the coup d'état was responsible for passing legislation in North Carolina that stripped African Americans of the vote through the grandfather clause, which allowed illiterate men to vote only if their grandfathers had voted before 1867. This disenfranchised black citizens, who had not been guaranteed the right to vote until the Fifteenth Amendment was ratified in 1870.

In the twentieth century, the story of what happened in 1898 was largely forgotten by the white community and barely mentioned in history books. That changed when the North Carolina General Assembly created the Wilmington Race Riot Commission to look into the incident. The commission's 2006 report, which includes photographs, maps, and charts, can be found at www.history.ncdcr.gov/1898-wrrc.

ACKNOWLEDGMENTS

My heartfelt thanks go out to Bill McBean, Lydia Chávez, Ursula Hegi, and Dennis Deas, who read early drafts and made valuable suggestions. Gail Hochman has been a constant support. Suzy Capozzi edited the book with clarity and insight. Thanks always to Frank, who makes me laugh.

Though I read widely in researching this book, certain works were particularly helpful. The story of the African American Siamese twins is covered in *Millie-Christine: Fearfully and Wonderfully Made* by Joanne Martell. An early and thoroughly researched account, *We Have Taken a City: The Wilmington Racial Massacre and Coup of 1898* by H. Leon Prather Sr., was published in 1984 and did not receive the attention it deserved. The official report of the 1898 Wilmington Race Riot Commission was invaluable.

ABOUT THE AUTHOR

BARBARA WRIGHT grew up in North Carolina and has lived all over the world: in France, in Korea, in El Salvador. She lives in Denver with her husband, and plays tennis and jazz piano whenever she can. Visit her online at www.barbarawrightbooks.com.